Merry Christmas, Cowboy

More Christmas romance from Janet Dailey

JANET DAILEY

Merry Christmas, Cowboy

KENSINGTON BOOKS
http://www.kensingtonbooks.com

KENSINGTON BOOKS are published by

Kensington Publishing Corp.
119 West 40th Street
New York, NY 10018

Library of Congress Card Catalogue Number: 2013936489

ISBN-13: 978-0-7582-8817-2
ISBN-10: 0-7582-8817-4

First Hardcover Printing: July 2013

10 9 8 7 6 5 4 3 2 1

Printed in the United States of America

Merry Christmas, Cowboy

Chapter 1

The huge pickup ahead of Paula Lewis's cop cruiser was spattered with frozen mud and straw, beat up but serviceable, with rugged tires intended for rough roads. Looked to her like it belonged to a cowboy. About all she could see of the man at the wheel were big shoulders and a Stetson.

He was probably in town to see the sights and raise a little hell. Denver was a magnet this time of year. The glittering Parade of Lights that kicked off the Christmas season started tonight. People came from all over to view the gorgeous floats and the bands marching past brick and stone buildings that were dressed up in lights too.

Solo for this shift, Paula was going to miss most of the excitement. Her usual partner had bailed on her, and there was no one available to sub for him. But other officers were in the area if she happened to need backup. Absently, she listened to the cop talk coming over the radio. Nothing noteworthy going on.

So far, her routine patrol around the civic center had been uneventful, which was good. The officers on the evening shift had been briefed on which streets were closed to vehicular traffic and other details. The parade would start in a few hours. It was already dark.

Paula braked when the pickup's taillights flashed again.

The driver kept slowing down, then speeding up again without ever going over the limit. A yellow light at the next intersection brought him to a complete halt. Paula gripped the steering wheel, rocked by the jolt of stopping short. She'd expected him to go through it. She shook her head. The cowboy was cautious. Or lost.

When he leaned sideways to peer at the street sign, another car swung to the left and went past her. Its headlights gave Paula a glimpse of the cowboy's chiseled profile above the turned-up collar of his denim jacket. The light turned red, and he straightened to look forward through the windshield again, tipping back the wide-brimmed hat he wore.

Hands still on the steering wheel, she glanced around. No minor mayhem or rowdy revelers yet. But the temporary placard restricting the cross street to pedestrians had been torn down. A white paper corner still dangled from a strip of tape attached to the lamppost.

Paula sighed. The light was taking forever to change.

For something to do, she ran the pickup's plates, taking in the information on the laptop while they both waited. The vehicle was registered to Zachary Bennett, age twenty-nine, in a county that was mostly ranches. No surprise there.

He seemed to be a law-abiding type. Clean record. No moving violations, not even an unpaid parking ticket.

Paula tapped a key to see more. His driver's license photo was dynamite. Strong jaw, sexy mouth. She glanced at the official description. Brown hair, blue eyes. Six foot three.

Stop it, she told herself. The Colorado DMV wasn't operating a dating service, and she was on the job.

Paula looked up when the light turned green, startled to see the pickup turn suddenly and fast, a shade too close to the curb. Fortunately, no one was standing there. But sign or no sign, Zachary Bennett had just gone down a street that was now closed. She would have to tactfully inform him of that fact and ask him to turn around.

She waited to follow him until the pickup stopped at the end of the block and eased into a parking spot, the engine still running. Despite the cold, there were plenty of people on the sidewalk. Couples and families headed toward the parade area to stake out good spots well in advance.

Paula pulled up beside the truck, looking at Zachary Bennett by the faint glow of the smartphone screen he was tapping. She rolled down the passenger side window of the cruiser and called to him. "Sir. *Sir.*"

He didn't seem to hear, absorbed in whatever was on the screen.

In her side mirror, she spotted a boy of about ten being yanked along by a big, goofy dog on a taut leash just before they crossed the street in front of her. Paula decided against using the loudspeaker, not wanting to get the dog barking or startle the kid. When they had passed, she switched on her roof lights for a few seconds. The brilliant flashes got her a bewildered stare from the cowboy. Now she had his attention.

Zachary Bennett rolled down his window. He made no attempt to hide the smartphone, holding it in the hand resting on the steering wheel. Paula leaned over to talk to him again. "Sir, are you aware that—"

"I pulled over and parked," he interrupted her. "I don't text and drive. Never have, never will."

He really hadn't done anything wrong, but she was still inclined to show him who was boss. As a general rule, Paula liked to finish her sentences.

"Glad to hear it. But that's not the issue." A few individuals glanced their way as she got out, walking around the cruiser to the pickup.

Paula was five-nine, but the height of the cab—and the man inside it—made her feel short. The winter Stetson, made of thick dark felt, framed a masculine face with strong cheekbones and intense blue eyes. The annoyed set of his jaw didn't keep her from thinking that he probably had a great smile. His face was lean and sun-weathered.

"So what did I do?"

She rested a gloved hand on her equipment belt. "You clipped the curb when you made that turn back there."

Technically, the huge tires had only kissed the concrete. But she could make the point that he had been going a little too fast if she wanted to.

He thought it over, staring down at her. "I don't think so." The reply was calm, almost cool. Zachary Bennett didn't seem like the type who'd argue with a cop, but she had a feeling he was stubborn. Cowboy attitude.

She cleared her throat. "I'm willing to let it go. But I do have to tell you that this street is temporarily closed off for the parade. Foot traffic only."

"Oh. Sorry." He stuck his head out of the window and looked back the way he'd come. "I didn't see a sign."

Paula acknowledged that with a nod. "There was a placard, but it was torn down. That's why I followed you. I'm not trying to give you a hard time or make a ticket quota."

"All right." He seemed okay with that, taking a moment to survey her from head to toe, but not in an obnoxious way.

There wasn't much to see, she thought. Dark uniform pants and a heavy jacket hid most of her slender body. Her long auburn hair was braided into a style that fit under her cap. Still, Paula was used to being flirted with.

A lot of guys thought female cops were fair game. She'd heard every dumb line there was. *What color are your eyes, officer? Take off that hat and let me see. You're too pretty for law enforcement.* And her personal favorite: *Don't tell me you take this job seriously.*

She did, though. Some people found that out the hard way.

Paula planted herself in her regulation-black shoes and stood tall. Close up, Zachary Bennett was too attractive for her peace of mind. Best to keep on doing the talking and not let him get started.

"You have to move your vehicle," Paula insisted. "No standing, no parking. Just go back. And be careful," she added. "It's a big night. I assume you're in town for the parade." She gestured toward the hurrying people.

"Nope."

"You're missing out. It's spectacular."

"So I hear," he said. "But I'm meeting a friend and I'm late."

Something told her the friend he was meeting was female. Instinct was a real bitch sometimes.

He smiled at her. "I hate to admit it but I'm lost. Maybe you can help."

Paula only nodded. The unexpected smile was a lot more effective than any line. Combined with the flash of humor in his blue eyes, it was downright unsettling.

"Okay."

He turned the smartphone toward her to show the map on the screen. "This damn thing keeps indicating a detour. The way it tells me to go will take me straight into the river—I'm sure of it. And it's way too cold for swimming."

Paula had to smile back. She glanced at the moving lines on the GPS map and up at him again. "Where exactly are you going?"

He told her, then added, "But I haven't been to Denver for a while. Maybe the app is right and I'm wrong."

"Actually, you are. That street's being repaired and there is a detour. Let me think for a sec. I'll try to keep you out of the river."

She gave him better directions, and he listened without asking for a repeat.

"Got it," he said when she'd finished. "Thanks, officer. I appreciate your assistance."

Paula had a feeling he'd find his way with no more trouble. Job done. And she'd satisfied her momentary curiosity about him.

"No problem. Enjoy your stay in Denver." She returned to the cruiser and got in, pulling ahead to let him turn around before she followed him back to the main street.

She turned left after he turned right. A marching band was coming her way, holding their instruments without playing them. The drum major turned and shouted an order that brought them to a bumping halt before he sorted them out into orderly ranks. He raised his baton and brought it down. In an instant, their uniforms brightened with tiny LEDs that shimmered in the night.

They fell into step and headed on.

Paula watched the illuminated band go down the closed street, marching to the tinkling melody of the xylophonist. The bare trees in the distance lit up with fairy lights as a brilliantly colored locomotive moved slowly into position behind other floats. She sighed. The magic was about to begin. Too bad she had no one to share it with.

Last time she'd been a spectator at the Parade of Lights, she'd been with her grandmother. Hildy Lewis had passed away two years ago and Paula never stopped missing her.

A call came over the radio. *Drunk and disorderly at Colfax and Ninth. Available units, please report.* Paula snapped out of it. She confirmed her location to the dispatcher and drove away.

She entered her apartment several hours later, slinging her wet jacket over a hook by the door. A light snow mixed with sleet had started toward the end of the parade, and Paula had been out in it.

Besides writing three summonses for petty mischief, she'd found the half-frozen drunk and arrested him for his own good. He was better off in a nice warm holding cell than out on the streets.

She made a cup of cocoa and traded her clunky shoes for shearling slippers, settling into a big pink armchair bequeathed to her by the former tenant. Paula groaned when her cell phone rang, debating whether to answer it.

She set down the cup and took the phone out of her shirt pocket, looking at the number. Edith Clayborne. Great old lady. Doing her best under difficult circumstances.

Paula had shown Edith the ropes the first time she'd come down to the station to pick up her teenaged grandson for a minor infraction. Brandon was a nice enough kid, but he was a handful and known to more than one officer. According to the social worker on the case, his parents' whereabouts were unknown, and Edith, a widow, was raising him alone.

The ringing stopped. Paula made a mental promise to check her voice mail in five minutes, just in case there was a genuine emergency. She'd given Edith her cell number for that reason. Paula had done youth outreach with at-risk teenagers like Brandon. She liked his grandmother and didn't want to see him end up in the overloaded juvenile justice system if she could help it.

She sipped her cocoa, warming her hands around the smooth cup. It was good to be home.

The phone rang again. She checked the number. Edith wasn't giving up. This time Paula answered it.

"Hi, honey," a raspy voice said cheerfully. "Hope I didn't catch you at a bad time."

"Hey, Edith. No, you didn't."

"Just thought I'd call."

Paula relaxed somewhat. It wasn't an emergency. But it was an interruption.

"Were you at the parade?" Edith asked.

"Yes. I just got home. Did you see it?"

"On TV. The floats are always so pretty." Edith paused. "I wanted to ask you about something—not Brandon. He's been behaving himself."

"Good. Keep him busy and keep him out of trouble."

"My thoughts exactly. That's why I got him to volunteer with me at the Christmas House."

Paula had seen a flyer for it in the station break room. A fine old mansion had been rescued from foreclosure and turned into a holiday attraction to benefit Denver-area charitable programs. Each room was a different theme. Candy-cane sculptures, elves, decorated trees, toy displays, the whole nine yards.

She set her cup aside. "When does it open?"

"We were shooting for the first of December."

"That's tomorrow," Paula said.

"The building and fire inspectors just certified the house today, so we can open just as soon as we get approval from our insurers. But there's a catch."

"Oh?"

"We have to have a security person on the premises."

"That could be expensive."

Edith sighed. "Well, the agent said we could use qualified volunteers if necessary."

Paula knew exactly where this conversation was going. She let Edith do the talking.

"All is not lost," the older woman said with dramatic emphasis. She did have a flair for it.

"Oh good."

"I know some nice retired men," Edith continued. Naturally.

"They work security for clothing and shoe stores, and

all we would need is two to cover the mornings and after-noons."

Grandpa guards. They didn't scare anyone, but the Christmas House didn't need scary staff.

"The problem is that no one is available in the eve-nings," Edith fretted. "And the plan was to stay open late on Fridays and Saturdays to attract as many visitors as possible."

"Makes sense."

"So do you think . . ."

Edith also was a master of the dramatic pause. Paula waited.

"Are you working nights?"

"Not next week."

"Is it possible . . ."

"Yes," Paula answered, laughing. "I could help you guys out for a few days. After that, I'm not sure. We don't get to pick and choose our holiday shifts—the sergeant does."

Edith heard only the positive part of the reply. She crowed with delight. "You're a doll! Wait until I tell the board! A real policewoman!"

"A moonlighting policewoman," Paula reminded her. "No uniform and no gun. And you have to keep looking for my replacement."

"Of course, of course," Edith said hurriedly. "Can you stop by the Christmas House tomorrow? You might have to pick your way through the ladders and sawdust, though."

"I don't care about stuff like that." Paula thought for a moment. As far as she knew, she would be working a day shift tomorrow. "I can come around six. How's that?"

"I'll be there with bells on. Can't wait to show you around and introduce you to everybody. Paula, thank you from the bottom of my heart. I can't believe you said yes."

Paula didn't quite believe it either. When Edith finally stopped talking and said good-bye, Paula got up to put her cup in the sink, peeking into the fridge on her way back into the living room. The white-wire shelves held a burger bag that had to have turned into a science experiment by now and two containers of plain yogurt.

She was too tired to order takeout and not inclined to cook for just herself. Around the holidays, living alone was no fun.

Paula drove her own car into the lot next to the Christmas House at ten to six, finding a slot among the many vehicles already parked. She took a few minutes to collect her thoughts, tired after a long day. Frazzled shoppers and oblivious drivers flooded downtown Denver. She'd dealt with everything from fender benders to arguments over parking spaces.

The tall windows of the mansion glowed with warm light on the first floor. Paula frowned as she peered through the wavy old glass. It didn't look like sawdust and ladders to her—it looked like a fancy reception in full swing. She'd thrown on old jeans and a ratty sweater after a quick stop at her apartment. That and her dusty sneakers would have to do. She was here.

A biting wind rushed through the car door when she opened it, tousling her hair. She decided to make a dash for the house without bothering with her jacket. If she had to check it at the door, it would take that much longer for her to leave. She didn't have to stay long. They had someone handling security for tonight—she remembered Edith saying so. But she hadn't said there would be a party.

She walked quickly out of the lot and ran up the stairs, entering through tall, unlocked doors into a swirl of bright lights and animated conversation. A few guests turned to smile her way, but most were occupied with admiring the décor and a bountiful buffet set out on cloth-draped tables.

Paula caught a glimpse of herself in a mirror and flinched. She would have fit in just fine with a younger crowd, but the people in attendance were of the generation that dressed up for an event like this. The attire ran to dark velvets and pearls on the beautifully coiffed women, suits and ties on the men with an occasional cashmere sweater. They had a well-heeled look and thank goodness for it. Paula suspected many if not all were the benefactors of the Christmas House.

She looked around for the volunteer types, hoping to find someone dressed as casually as she was. Maybe they were in the kitchen with the caterers. She wouldn't mind joining them. Maybe she could swipe a knee-length apron as a disguise.

Edith came forward through the crowd, her blond hair freshly stacked and sprayed, her bracelets jingling as she waved. Her plump figure was encased in turquoise brocade, and she wore eye shadow to match. Paula smiled. Edith's taste in clothes was far from grandmotherly.

"Paula! Welcome!"

"Hi, Edith. The house looks beautiful. So do you."

"Thanks, honey. Your hair is amazing. I don't think I've ever seen you with it down. Who styled it?"

"The wind."

"Oh," Edith said, then, "Why are you looking at me like that?"

Paula steered her out to the front hall. "I didn't know there was going to be a party," she replied in a low voice. "I would have changed."

"I thought I told you. Oh gosh, I'm sorry. But you look fine."

Paula laughed. "I wish."

Edith gave her a contrite look. "There are taffeta skirts

in the costume closet you could borrow. Our lady elves made their own. There goes one."

Paula heard the skirt rustle by before she turned and took in the neon-green plaid the woman wore. "That's okay," she told Edith. "Let's get back to the party."

She shook a lot of hands and met nice people who didn't seem to notice what she was wearing at all. The conversation centered on the house and how much had been accomplished and what remained to be done.

Plenty, by the sound of it. The check-writers didn't look like they had a lot of experience with hammers and staple guns.

Most of the guests gathered for a house tour when the punchbowl was empty and the food had been served, but Paula begged off, taking Edith aside.

"I can get here by three tomorrow. It's my day off," she told her. "I thought I'd do a little Christmas shopping, then come over and really look at the house before I start my shift. I can't wait to see the theme rooms."

"Whatever you want," Edith said. "I'll take you around myself. Brandon will be here tomorrow. This isn't his kind of party."

Paula looked at the guests milling around. She didn't need to ask his grandmother why a fifteen-year-old would skip it. "How's he doing?"

"He's a teenager. Up one day, down the next," Edith replied. "He's a good kid. But holidays are hard. He keeps hoping to hear from his mom or dad. I don't think it's going to happen."

"That's not easy, but don't let him take it out on you," Paula reminded her. "You're all he's got."

"He doesn't, Paula. I think he knows that."

Paula returned as promised the next day. There were only a few cars in the parking lot now.

This time Paula took her coat. She wouldn't be leaving until late, and the radio weatherman had said something about a cold front coming in.

It was nice not to be tired. Her shopping, not that she had much to do, was complete. A sweet-treats basket for her next-door neighbor, gag gifts for college friends who'd moved away, and several department-store cards just in case. She could always use them to shop for herself if she didn't give them away. Edith and Brandon took a little thought. She hadn't decided on anything for either of them.

She went up the front stairs, noticing that the wrought-iron railings were adorned with fresh pine garlands and each first-floor window now sported a wreath with a big red bow. Whoever put them up had left a long ladder against the exterior wall. The Christmas House was getting there.

A toy sleigh filled with flyers had been set in a sheltered spot by the door. Paula bent down and took a bunch.

Edith Clayborne opened the door just as Paula straightened. "What are you doing?"

"I'm going to hand these out to colleagues with kids. And colleagues with no kids. Gotta get the word out." Paula slipped the flyers into her tote bag.

Edith made a face. "Don't I know it. We might have more volunteers than visitors today." She peered out from behind the door as if she thought there might be more of the latter coming down the street. There was no one.

"We can change that," Paula said briskly. "Larimer Square is a popular place for tourists, and you're right on the border between it and downtown." She looked up at the wide fan window over the double doors. "For starters, the House needs a sign. A big one."

"That's in the works," Edith assured her. "We found a woodworker who restores historic houses, and he donated his time and materials. He's delivering it today with a friend."

"Excellent." Paula unwound her scarf. "Mind if I come in?"

Edith chuckled and stepped aside. "Please do. We may need you for more than security. I'm thinking I talked you into the wrong job."

Paula slipped off her coat and hung it up in the entryway closet, eyeing Edith's holiday outfit with amusement. "Nice sweater."

"Thanks, honey. The reindeer nose in the middle lights up." She demonstrated.

It even blinked. Paula laughed. "The kids will love it." She tugged her own plain sweater down over her hips. "So show me everything, starting from here."

Edith gestured to an older man in a chambray shirt and bolo tie sitting at a card table, counting out bills and change into a decorated box with an open lid. "That's Norville," she whispered. "I don't want to distract him. But he's handling the door for today."

Paula looked at the admission fees on the placard by the box. Five dollars for adults, two-fifty for kids. A family of four or more could get in for ten. Seemed reasonable. But the lightweight box was no place to keep cash. She made a mental note to address that issue later.

"How late can you stay tonight?" Edith asked.

"Until closing time. And after," Paula added. "We should sit down and talk once I have a better idea of how things work."

The older woman beamed at her. "What else could I persuade you to do?"

"I looked at my calendar last night. It's not as full as I thought. Once you find another security volunteer, I could probably help with community relations, maybe publicity. People can find you online, right?"

Edith hesitated. "Maybe by tomorrow. Our Web site designer says we don't have enough photos. She might be stopping by later to take some. When we finish the displays, that is."

Maybe and *might* weren't Paula's favorite words. "Is there a task list?"

"Somewhere," Edith answered ruefully. "Anything you want to do is going to help, honey."

Paula wasn't that sure. "I guess I could paint pinecones or something. Just don't ask me to sew." A delicious aroma was filling the air. "What smells so good?"

"Gingerbread cookies. Come into the kitchen."

Paula followed Edith down the hall, glancing into the room where the reception had been held. She stopped to look when someone in the kitchen yelled for Mrs. Clayborne, and the older woman went ahead.

"I'll be there in a minute, Edith," she called after her.

There were a number of trees in the room, none of them real. Volunteers in jeans and sneakers—Paula was among her own kind at last—had finished decorating two and were starting on the third. A handsome partridge sat in a faux pear tree and two doves adorned the top of a feathery pine. At the moment, beady-eyed fowls were being wired into a blue spruce.

A college girl turned around and saw Paula. "Hi there. Meet Fifi, Mimi, and Gigi."

Paula laughed. "Three French hens. I get it. Keep on clucking."

"We will. There's a lot more to do," the girl replied. "Twelve Days of Christmas, twelve trees. Nine to go."

She stepped back and joined her group to confer as Paula moved on.

The spicy scent of gingerbread lured her into the kitchen. Edith was admiring trays of cookies set out to cool and chatting with the baker, a thin man in a white cloth jacket and cap. She introduced Paula and handed her a basket of broken ones to sample.

"We lacquer the perfect cookies once they're cooled and iced," the baker explained as Paula nibbled. "They last longer that way. These are for a snow scene."

In a twist on tradition, the gingerbread men and women were on skis, their roly-poly shapes in downhill-racer position. Several young assistants with icing bags were making smiles and buttons on wax paper for practice.

"Wonderful. What fun." Paula finished her very tasty sample. Edith *toodle-ooed* her way to the door and she followed.

"Those kids are from the culinary program at the trade school," Edith said once they were back in the hall. "I guess they're not exactly kids," she amended. "They're older than Brandon, although not by much. I was hoping he'd meet some new pals here."

Paula nodded, not wanting to get into it. Edith had told her before that a few of Brandon's so-called friends were several steps ahead of him on the wrong path.

The rest of the tour was fast. Paula was amazed by the variety of the themed rooms but was unable to take in every detail. But there would be time for that.

As they walked toward the front door, they heard the rattle and clank of a ladder being moved. It was visible through the fan window and so were the workboots of the man who'd just climbed it.

A large flat shape was being handed up to him.

Edith turned excitedly to Paula. "The sign is here!"

"Can we go out and see?" Paula asked. "Wait a sec. I brought a camera. Let's get a few shots. The Web designer could use 'em." She went around Edith to the entryway closet and retrieved her tote bag.

The older woman was already at a side door that Paula hadn't noticed. "Get me a jacket," she called. "Any jacket, I don't care."

Paula dragged her coat off the hanger and picked a colorful fleece thing for Edith.

"You're psychic. That happens to be mine."

Halfway bundled up, they went out and around the mansion.

"There's Jake," Edith said as they approached the front stairs. The man by the door had just let go of the sign. His assistant, a skinny kid in a knit cap, was beside him, bracing the ladder.

Jake, a blond guy in a padded flannel overshirt and baggy jeans, turned at the sound of his name as the women mounted the stairs.

"Paula, this is Jake Nilsson, our woodworker. And I don't know your name," Edith said to his assistant in a bubbly voice.

"Hank," was the mumbled reply.

"You got it all right?" Jake asked the man at the top of the ladder.

He was the tallest and strongest of the three, with dark hair that curled over the collar of a worn denim jacket. Paula couldn't see his face. Way up there, he handled the large, newly painted wooden sign as if it didn't weigh much, but he was careful.

"Yeah," he answered without turning his head, his back to all of them as he concentrated on getting metal hooks into eyebolts that had already been installed.

"Maybe we should skip the introductions," Paula whispered to Edith.

"Goodness, yes. I talk too much, don't I?"

Paula noted Jake Nilsson suppressing a smile. But he didn't take his eyes off the man at the top of the ladder until the sign was safely in place.

His friend gave it a tap. It swung slightly, then hung still.

"That's not going anywhere," he said with satisfaction.

He stepped down from rung to rung, turning to them when he was nearly at the bottom.

Paula just stared. She knew that face. He looked at her without recognizing her, then started to take off the tool belt slung around his hips. He handed it to Hank. A flat clip holding business cards and a photo and a twenty-dollar bill fell out at Paula's feet. She bent to pick it up and handed it to Zach.

"Thanks." He tucked the clipped things into his shirt pocket.

Next to his heart, she thought. Meaning the photo of a pretty girl in the snow somewhere. Stood to reason he would have one.

He was smiling at Edith.

"Hello. I believe your name is Zach Bennett," she chirped.

"Yes, ma'am."

"Zach volunteered a week ago," Edith explained. "Everyone, this is Paula Lewis, from the Denver police department. She volunteered to handle security in the evenings for the next few days. But we hope that won't be all. She's full of good ideas. Paula could be with us through December. Isn't that nice? We are so blessed to have you all."

Paula smiled in an embarrassed way. She wasn't about to remind Zach Bennett that they'd met before. But his intense blue eyes narrowed as he studied her. He looked at her hair first, then the rest of her.

She pulled her coat closed and pushed tumbling auburn locks away from her cheeks. Heat flamed as a slow smile came over his face.

"Hello, officer," he said.

"Oh, do you two know each other?" Edith asked brightly.

"Not personally."

Jake looked between the two of them. "What?" he said to Zach. "Did she give you a ticket?"

Zach shook his head. "I took a wrong turn the night I drove in to meet you. She helped me find my way."

"I don't believe you," Nilsson said dryly. "You never get lost, and you always drive like you're on ranch roads. You must have done something, cowboy."

"He didn't." Paula felt a little funny defending him to his buddy.

Amusement and annoyance warred in Zach's gaze. "You heard her, Jake. I didn't do anything."

"Yeah?" Nilsson winked at Paula. "That's not like you."

Chapter 2

Out of breath after climbing the stairs to the attic an hour later, Edith unlocked a door and pushed it open. Paula followed her in. A blast of chilly air and sunlight made them both blink. The shadows of late afternoon hadn't reached the top floor of the old mansion.

An ancient iron bed frame took up half of the small room. It was heaped with a generous pile of colorful quilts and pillows.

"I brought all this from home. I thought it would be nice to have a place for volunteers to relax or even catch a nap. Some of them show up before breakfast and work past midnight," Edith explained.

Paula nodded. "You really have a great team."

"They deserve a little pampering," Edith said, shivering in her sweater. "Brrr. That cold front is here. I can feel the draft. There's a space heater if you need it."

"Okay. Thanks."

"And you don't have to work on the bed." Edith pointed to a table with a lamp, as if Paula wouldn't have noticed it without her guidance. "There's that."

"I'll manage. It's only for an hour." She'd asked Edith for a quiet space to jot down her notes and a tentative schedule.

The older woman handed her the plans for the theme rooms and a list of volunteers. "Ask Norville where I am when you come back downstairs. The second I stop, someone needs me."

Paula could remember her grandmother telling her the same thing. The memory was poignant.

She went to the window and looked out. The mansion's top floor was high enough for a good view of the historic part of Denver.

It was the parking lot below that interested her more. Zach's pickup straddled two spaces near the gate. The mud was gone. The dark paint gleamed in the fading winter light. She noticed a tool chest made of diamond-patterned steel that hadn't been there before, a professional model, padlocked and bolted to either side of the back.

Edith came over. "What's out there?"

"Zach Bennett's pickup."

"Oh my. I guess they needed the space to unload the sign," Edith said absently. "Did you really meet him before?"

Paula nodded. "Random traffic stop. I never expected to see him again."

"Well, Zach Bennett is certainly worth looking at," the older woman teased.

"True enough," Paula said warily. "And it's very nice of him to volunteer with Jake, but that's not why I'm here. Besides, the sign is finished and installed."

"That doesn't mean he won't be around."

Paula didn't answer.

"Okay," Edith said. "I can take a hint." She shut up.

For five whole seconds.

"Jake told me he made the sign to last," the older woman sighed. "I just hope we make it through the season. Did you get a good picture of it?"

"Several." The camera was in her tote bag. Later for photo sharing, Paula thought. She wanted to get to work.

"We don't have the house indefinitely. The board would like to keep it going year after year, but after January, who knows?"

"Let's just think about what we can do right now," Paula said, turning away from the window. She set the tote bag on the table and eased herself into the creaky chair, switching on the small lamp.

"All right, honey. I have things to do too. I'm heading for the Snowbunny Suite."

Paula took out the plans. "Second floor, north side, two doors down from the landing?"

"That's right. Want me to leave the door open?"

Paula nodded as she spread out her paperwork. Edith left, clattering down the stairs. The echoes faded into a silence that allowed Paula to concentrate on the task of organizing, which she liked. Lists, plans, schedules were definitely her thing.

An hour passed before she frowned and turned toward the window. A loud conversation had started below— teenagers, by the sound of it. Joking, cursing, all-around full of themselves. Paula got up to see, switching off the table lamp.

There was no curtain to hide behind, but she doubted the boys below would notice her standing behind the glass. They had already triggered the motion-sensor lights illuminating the parking lot. Paula realized that Edith's grandson was with them.

There were two others she didn't know. By her guess, they were a few years older than Brandon. One had a straggly blond mustache she could see from up here and a lip piercing that glinted in the harsh light. The other had a black Mohawk and blotchy skin. Probably acne.

The blond boy took out a pack of cigarettes and tapped

out one for himself with a practiced move, sticking it in his mouth before he offered the pack to his pals.

Brandon hesitated—she knew him well enough to know he didn't smoke or at least he didn't do it around his grandmother. He took a cigarette when the second boy did, huddling with the others around the flicked lighter.

Paula was tempted to sic Edith on him. *Choose your battles,* she told herself. This one wasn't hers. Brandon coughed and waved at the smoke, as if it were bothering his eyes and not his throat. Faker.

The boys walked aimlessly through the lot and stopped at Zach's pickup, the largest vehicle in it. They leaned against the side and slid down, crouching to stay out of the wind.

The idle talk continued but not so loudly. Still, a trick of the wind carried the gist of it to her high above.

Paula saw a long shadow come through the parking lot gate and recognized the man who made it. Zach strode quickly toward the driver's side door, auto-unlocking the cab.

The beep startled Brandon, who stood up. The other two scrambled away and left him there. But Paula could still see them on the other side of the next vehicle. She edged closer to the window to hear better.

Zach looked about as surprised as Brandon did. "What are you doing there?"

"Nothing." The teenager tossed the cigarette away, still coughing.

Paula wondered why he didn't back away.

Zach took a jacket out of the cab and put it on, keeping an eye on Brandon. Then he swung himself up into the back of the pickup, lifting the padlock on the tool chest as if he wanted to make sure it hadn't been tampered with.

"Nice truck," Brandon said.

"Not new but I like it. Had it a long time," Zach answered. The terse exchange stopped for a few seconds while he climbed back out.

"I was just looking at it," Brandon ventured.

The other two boys, who were feeling bold or maybe just cold, came forward. "Yeah. Us too. We're together."

Zach shrugged, unimpressed. The three boys looked like pipsqueaks next to him. "So why are you hanging around a parking lot? None of you look old enough to drive."

"He is." Brandon jerked a thumb at the oldest of the boys.

Zach took in that reply as the two others stepped forward. Then they made a run for it, laughing like hyenas. Brandon looked after them and then at Zach.

"Honestly, we didn't do anything."

"I hope you have a reason to be here," was all Zach said.

"My grandma's inside."

Paula was glad Brandon's obnoxious friends hadn't stuck around to hear him say something so naïve.

"Really."

"Her name is Edith. You can ask her if you don't believe me."

"Oh." Zach's gruff tone altered but not by much. "What did you say your name was?"

"Brandon."

Zach gestured him away from the truck. "After you. Let's go inside."

Paula watched the two of them head through the gate at the front of the Christmas House. Slight as he was, Brandon seemed to be about half the size of Zachary Bennett. But he hadn't backed down or run away, and he'd answered honestly when questioned.

She had to give him credit for all three. Paula decided not to tell Edith she'd seen him smoking.

She gathered up her things and headed downstairs. The hustle and bustle of construction got louder as she reached the second floor and then the first. There was Norville with the cashbox. The old man was chatting with a young dad in charge of several kids. Zach and Brandon were nowhere in sight.

"They all yours?" Norville chuckled. He looked over his glasses at the children.

"The four with red hair are," the dad answered. "The other two might as well be—they're over at our house so much."

Paula stood in the hall, listening for a moment before she went to find Edith.

"I see the resemblance," Norville said, peering up at the younger man. "That hair and them freckles do match. Now, I have to tell you that we ain't but half finished with some rooms. So if you want to come back another night—"

There were wails of disappointment from the children, who Paula guessed ranged in age from kindergarteners to first and second graders.

"Nope," said the dad with a laugh. "How much is it for all of us?"

Norville turned the placard toward the group. "Ten for the whole family. The other two youngsters are included."

"I have a better idea." Paula walked over and stood on Norville's side of the table. "As our first visitors of the evening, how about free admission?"

The dad had a twenty halfway out of his wallet. "Seriously?"

"If you come in free tonight, you can come back another night and see all the displays. Bring your friends."

The twenty went back into the wallet. "I like the way you think," the dad said.

"Hold your horses, kids," Norville said with a twinkle

in his eye. "I have to stamp the back of your hands so we know you didn't sneak in here."

The children obliged, thrilled to get a star each.

"You tell your mommas that'll wash right off in the bath," he added, setting aside the stamp and inkpad.

Off to the side, Paula caught a glimpse of Brandon, who gave her a guilty look. There was no way he had seen her at the upstairs window, but Zach could still be looking to talk to Edith. In a teenager's mind, a parent/guardian/ friend of the family was in the same camp. Paula was inclined to stall on what could turn into a prickly conversation.

"Let me find someone who can take you around, sir," she told the young father quickly. "You look like you could use a little help."

Paula bent down to murmur in Norville's ear. "Where did Edith go? Is she still in the Snowbunny Suite?"

"Here she comes."

Edith approached, not seeing Brandon, who faded back into the wallpaper. Teenagers had the knack. Paula had been good at disappearing herself.

"Hi, kids!" Edith said. "Are you all one group? Oh my."

Paula provided a fast explanation, and Edith instantly took the family under her wing. She led them away as Norville shook his head at Paula. "Now why'd you do that?"

"For good luck. If six kids tell their friends, that's at least six more families with one or two kids, maybe more, plus their friends, coming through the door. If they tell their aunts and uncles and grandparents, and we get some couples and single people, too, that cashbox will fill up fast. Do the math."

Norville chuckled. "It does kinda make sense if you don't think about it too hard."

She unfolded a chair and took her place next to Norville. "How much do you keep on hand to make change?"

"About a hundred, all told." Norville patted the lid of the box. "Ones, fives, tens, a couple of twenties. My theory is that folks with kids usually have the right amount handy to save their sanity."

"Maybe so. But I'd like to keep it all safe. Maybe we can build a better box. I wonder where Zach Bennett got to," she said.

"That tall fella? Last I saw, he was in the kitchen with the baker lady."

Paula felt a tiny, unwanted twinge of jealousy. It had been a baker man when she'd been there.

"He musta heard you mention his name, Paula. There he is."

She looked to where Norville nodded and saw Zach coming through the kitchen door behind a white-haired woman with an apron tied around her generous middle. Paula remembered her as one of Edith's friends from the senior center. Her pointless crush on him—she had to admit that she had the beginnings of one—was safe for now.

The second Zach saw Paula over the baker's shoulder, his blue eyes fixed on her. He handed over a basket of glazed gingerbread cookies as the baker thanked him and went down the hall with it. He headed for the card table.

"How are we doing?" he asked. The question was general, not directed specifically to either Norville or her. But his gaze was still on Paula.

"Thanks to her, we haven't made a cent," grumbled Norville. "She let seven people in free. Said it was good luck or something."

Zach caught the old man's wink and grinned. "Was that the group I saw go by with Edith?"

"Yes," Paula replied. "Hey, I'm glad you stopped by. I

was hoping you hadn't left yet." She held up her security checklist. It would be nice to get the first thing on it taken care of as soon as possible. "I have another project for you."

"Okay." His deep voice had a noncommittal ring. That wasn't a yes or a no.

"Nothing difficult, of course." She decided to go for it. "You brought woodworking tools, right?"

Act innocent, she told herself. He didn't need to know she'd spied on him from on high. If he'd opened the padlock on the steel toolbox, she could have given him an inventory of his gear.

"Yes. They're in the back of my truck. What do you have in mind?"

Paula indicated the cashbox. "I think we could use a bigger one. This is too easy to swipe."

"I never take my eyes off it," Norville protested.

"But you're not always going to be here," Paula told him.

"Where's your faith in mankind?" the old man wanted to know.

That slow smile stole across Zach's face. She hoped he wasn't going to tell on her for pulling him over without much of a reason.

"Things happen around the holidays," she said to Norville. "It's no reflection on you. So what I was thinking—"

Zach lifted the cashbox. "We can't bolt this to a metal card table. I'm thinking you need a new table with a built-in drop slot. Box above, box below, if you follow me."

"Yes, but—"

He didn't seem to be listening to her. "The cash you don't need could go into the lower box from time to time. Keep some back to make change. We would need, oh, planks, sawhorses, some scrap wood for the two boxes. Easy to do."

"Sounds good," Norville said with enthusiasm. "No one can steal a whole darn table, Paula."

"No. They can't." She didn't bother going into her idea. It wasn't as good.

"Want me to start now?" Zach asked her.

She couldn't really tell if he was kidding or not. "Do we have the lumber?"

"I think I can find some."

He turned as the outer door opened. Several rosy-cheeked kids, middle-schoolers, blew in with the wind at their backs. They stopped to hold the door for their parents.

"Hey, more customers," Norville said happily. "Paula, you could be right about the good luck."

She wasn't going to argue with that. The kids ran to the table, unwinding scarves and jamming hats in their pockets. The parents and a solo friend paid the full admission.

Norville took the ten and the five, putting them in their respective compartments. Hands stamped, the group sorted themselves out just as Edith turned a corner with the redheaded family.

"You're just in time," she called. "These folks got a little bit of a head start, but I can show you what they saw when we're all done. Join us."

Paula turned to speak to Zach, but he had gone. She sat down again. Norville watched the door as if he expected hordes of visitors to burst through, but the front hall was quiet again, except for the Christmas carol the old man was humming.

The heavy tread of workboots broke the near silence. Zach reappeared holding several long planks balanced on one shoulder, two sawhorses over the other, and a canvas bag of tools in that hand.

"Should I start now?" he asked.

Paula knew she'd been one-upped by him. She didn't

mind all that much. Not if she got to look at hardworking brawn while she ate her humble pie.

"Sure," she said. "I mean, I'm not in charge around here, but sure."

"I'll take that as a yes. Everyone else seems to be improvising."

"That is a fact," Norville said dryly. "I can help, Zach, if Paula don't mind keeping an eye on the money."

"Not at all," she said.

She sat back with her arms crossed over her chest and watched the two men put together a tabletop in record time. Zach notched two planks for the drop slot and sawed the pieces for two boxes. Norville tapped in finishing nails at the corners and added hinges and small latches to the lids.

"That about does it," Zach said. "Rough and ready, but she's done."

"We can bang everything into place right now and ask Brandon to put on a coat of primer tonight," Norville said with satisfaction. "She'll be ready to paint by tomorrow."

Paula noticed a faint change in Zach's expression at the mention of Brandon. She still didn't know if he had verified the boy's relationship to Edith yet.

"Where is that kid? Brandon?" Norville called. His creaky voice echoed in the front hall. He waited for several seconds. "I don't think he left, not without his grandma."

"I wouldn't know," Zach said. He unfolded the sawhorses and set the planks on top of them, using flat brackets to bolt them together. "Hmm. We could save time and paint if Edith has fabric to put over the table part."

"Edith?" Norville asked. "She has enough blasted fabric and rickrack and glitter to open a craft store. I helped her carry in a dozen bags this morning."

Paula nodded in agreement. "I'll ask her when she comes back," she told Zach.

Enough time had passed for the first and second group to have visited all the theme rooms. Paula could hear the laughter mixed in with oohs and aahs. Edith's voice floated over the others. She was in her element, telling the children everything they wanted to know.

Slowly, the children and adults from the two groups began to drift back into the front hall.

Norville took up his place at the original card table and put on an official air. "Y'all looked like you enjoyed yourselves."

The redheaded dad shepherded his offspring and their buddies toward the door. "Hate to leave. But these kids are having a sugar rush. The bakery lady let them have anything they wanted."

"Uh-oh," Paula said.

"Not a problem," the man assured her. "They had dinner before we came."

The kids were looking curiously at Zach. "Are you making a display?" one asked.

"Nope. Just a table. We need a bigger one for in here."

"That's for sure," the man told him. "I'm featuring the Christmas House on my blog. Here's my card. I'll post the review tonight."

He fumbled in a pocket and took out a couple of cards, handing one to Norville and one to Paula.

"Holy cow. You're Denver Dave?" she asked, looking up at him. "Why didn't you tell us?"

"I like to go incognito. And I usually don't get recognized. But yes, I am the one and only Dave Friedrich, famous freeloader and events reviewer," he said, making a joke out of it.

Norville's gray eyebrows went up. Zach paid attention without saying anything.

"Seriously, we had no idea," Paula said. "You really were our first visitors. I'm so glad you liked everything."

On autopilot, she walked the excited kids and the dad to the door. "Come back again," she said.

"We will," the kids chorused. "We made him promise."

Dave gave her a sheepish grin in farewell. "Had to. They can't wait to see the rest."

The second group took a little longer to depart. The youngsters tumbled over each other as their parents struggled to get them back into their mittens, hoods, and scarves.

"I'm hot!" one complained.

"You won't be when you get outside," a mother said.

Zach stopped working to watch the chaotic exodus, his hammer in his hand. "I don't know how moms and dads do it," he said, almost to himself, when everyone had gone.

"One day at a time," Norville replied. "And on the last day, when they're grown and gone, you wish you could do it all over again. Then you come to your senses."

Zach laughed. "How many kids did you have, Norville?"

"Two sons and a daughter. They do me proud, but I'm glad it's just me and the wife now. We like having the house to ourselves." He looked at his watch. "Speaking of that, she was expecting me home an hour ago. Mind if I head out, Paula?"

"Go ahead. See you tomorrow night."

"You bet." He rose stiffly and went to the front closet to get his coat.

In another few minutes, Paula was alone with Zach Bennett.

Chapter 3

Zach didn't say anything as he concentrated on finishing the table, smoothing down the rough edges of the cut planks with a piece of sandpaper. Paula watched. He had great hands, long-fingered and strong, with big knuckles that had their share of nicks and scrapes.

"Is that what you do for a living?"

"Carpentry? Not really," he answered, not looking at her. "Most of the time I help run the family ranch. It's hard to make a go of just that, so we all do other things when we can."

"*We* meaning . . . ?"

"My older brother Sam. He just got married to a New York girl who loves Colorado. They go betwixt and between. And my sister Annie is a ski instructor in Aspen. But the ranch is the home place. My parents still live there."

"Sounds nice."

"It's beautiful. How about yourself? You from Denver? Sisters and brothers?"

Let's get it over with, she thought as she looked at him.

"I was the only one. My parents died in a car crash when I was little. My Grandma Hildy raised me. Born and raised in Denver, and never been much of anywhere else."

"Me neither, except around the west coast. I do seasonal installations all over around the holidays. Jake happened to call me to help him make that sign. Otherwise I don't see him too much this time of year."

"So I can count myself lucky that I pulled you over that night."

He raised his dark head and looked at her. "Think so?"

The blunt question stopped her. "I was just making conversation. I didn't mean anything particular by that."

"Just asking." He returned to the tedious work of sanding, caressing the wood absently with his palm.

"Any splinters?"

"Not yet. This is good wood."

Maybe it wasn't the best idea to watch him work. His attention to detail made Paula feel almost ignored, although he was talking to her. It was the coordinated rhythm of man and muscle that was getting to her. Easy strokes. Nice and steady.

Without knowing it, she sighed. Zach looked up. "You tired?"

"A little. But I want to stay late and talk to Edith. There are a lot of things to figure out. As you can see, security is my department."

Zach nodded. "Tell me about that Brandon kid."

She sat up and looked around, listening. "I think he's still here. Anyway, there's not much to tell. He is Edith's grandson—"

Paula stopped. She'd given herself away by saying he was probably still here.

"I saw you at the upstairs window," Zach said. "I guess you must have heard some of the conversation, if you could call it that."

Busted. Paula looked straight at him without apologizing. "Yes, I did. I was working up there."

"What? Doing surveillance? This neighborhood isn't that bad."

"I was going over plans and looking at the volunteer list," Paula replied coolly. "Someone has to make sure all the little pieces fit."

"You could have filled me in. The mood I was in, I might have said something stupid and insulted Edith. She's a nice lady."

"Zach—look, I'm sorry. I did think of looking for you, but there were people around and I had to help Norville. Besides, I figured you were smart enough to understand once Brandon explained himself."

"He seemed all right," Zach admitted. "The other two got my back up."

"I never saw them before, but I do know Brandon."

That reply left a lot unsaid. He could read between the lines if he wanted to.

"The way he acted, I thought he was looking to steal something. Then I changed my mind. But even so—"

"Just so you know, his parents haven't been part of his life for years, and Edith is doing her damnedest to raise him right. Sometimes he slips up." Paula held up a hand. The quiet sound of sneakers on wood floors reached her. "Brandon?" she called.

The slight boy stepped into view but didn't come into the hall. "I didn't lie to you, dude," he said to Zach.

Zach considered his words before replying. "I got the wrong idea. That's all I can say."

Brandon stayed silent. He didn't look to Paula for support.

"For the record, I'm sorry," Zach continued. "But you were hanging around the only truck I have and it's how I get to work."

"You asked me what I was doing and I told you. Nothing."

Zach cleared his throat. "I never got away with that for an answer at your age." He paused for a beat. "Look, let's just drop it."

"Okay."

Paula could hear the hurt in the boy's voice. But she had to be a little tough with him.

"Brandon, your friends didn't help the situation. I don't want to see them around the Christmas House again." It was the truth.

"They're not my friends," he said. The answer came a little too fast. "Just kids I know. Did he tell you about them or were you watching from somewhere?"

"I saw them for myself," she said. "By chance, but I am supposed to be in charge of security around here. Are they in your school? They looked older than you," she said.

"I don't know how old they are."

Paula exchanged a look with Zach when the boy heard his grandmother's cheerful voice calling him.

"Can I go?" he asked her.

Paula nodded. "Are you coming back tomorrow?"

"Maybe."

Paula was online, part of her early morning ritual with coffee. She looked up Denver Dave. It seemed too soon for him to have posted anything, but he'd said he would.

The Web page loaded. There was his review, front and center.

> *Denver's latest and greatest attraction is about to open! Be sure to treat yourself to a visit to the Christmas House near Larimer Square—and keep in mind that you have to go more than once to see it all. I took my four kids plus two pint-size pals for a sneak peek at how the magic gets made last night, and we're going back. Friendly staffers and unique displays make this first-ever seasonal delight a must for families, couples, and anyone who loves the holidays. Every room fea-*

*tures a different theme and imagination rules.
Admission? More than reasonable. Ten bucks
for the whole family and five singles for the sin-
gle. You can't go wrong. Just go. The Christmas
House gets our coveted Five Mittens Award for
December fun. Don't miss it!*

Paula let out a whoop of joy and sat back. That was a
rave—and there were driving directions and a map in a
sidebar. Everyone read Denver Dave. She blew a kiss at the
little photo, which didn't look anything like him. Paula
downed the last of her lukewarm coffee and got ready to
go to work.

This Christmas House thing could turn out to be just
what she needed. She'd been wanting to meet new people,
and half of Denver would be coming through the doors
after that review. Paula knew how easy it was to eat, sleep,
and breathe the job—and never interact with anyone but
other cops.

She'd found herself doing just that. The best officers
could get too tough and hopelessly cynical. She didn't want
it to happen to her.

The sergeant assigned her to foot patrol downtown. She
tipped her hat to him. It was a beautiful day, even if it was
cold. Paula started out at the far end of 16th Street and fell
into a steady pace. The shop windows—upscale chains
and boutiques alike—were dressed in their holiday best.
None had anything on the Christmas House. She couldn't
wait to get back there.

By the time she did, it was early in the evening. There
was a line of people on the stairs, going up slowly. Kids
clung to their parents' hands, and Paula noted several
young couples who'd chosen the House for a date.

"I'm not cutting in," she assured the woman waiting

with her daughter just outside the mansion's doors. "I work here."

The woman smiled. "Lucky you."

Paula ducked in, hurrying to Norville. He sat behind the new table, which had been draped with holiday fabric almost to the floor and lavishly trimmed. Someone had covered the box with the same fabric and added a wooden candy-cane handle.

"Wow. This looks a lot better than that old card table." She slid out of her coat and settled it on the folding chair beside Norville.

"Edith did the decorating," Norville replied. "Give that woman a glue gun and she'll take over the world."

"Are we admitting people in groups?" she asked.

"Have to. That blogger fella got folks interested. Quite a turnout."

"Maybe we should send Brandon out there with free cups of cocoa."

"What is it with you and giving things away?" the old man asked. But his voice was kind.

"If people get cold, they won't stay," she replied. "A few packages of instant cocoa aren't going to break the bank. Where is Brandon?"

Then she remembered that he hadn't promised to come back.

"Haven't seen him. Line's starting to move."

There was a squeeze of puffy jackets blocking the door. A young volunteer went over to help, getting the eager kids into some kind of line.

Norville flipped up the lid of the new cashbox. "Let me show you real quick how this works. The top part lifts out." He demonstrated. "And there's the drop slot under that. Zach said he got Brandon to help him make a locking drawer for the bottom part. Makes it easier to get at the money and still keeps it safe."

"Oh." Paula looked at Norville, a little surprised. "Who has the key?"

"Girl, don't you ever stop being suspicious? I have one and Edith has the other."

"Excellent. And very clever," she said to him. "How many?" she asked the woman she'd seen on her way in.

"Just me and my daughter."

"Family admission is ten." Paula lowered her voice. "But let's make it five, since there's only two of you."

Norville kicked her under the table, then stamped the little girl's hand with a star and did the same for her mother. Paula kept a straight face. Before the next visitors stepped up, she explained, "For luck. We have to keep it going."

"That was nice of you to teach Brandon a little carpentry."

Zach shrugged but he didn't seem to mind Paula's praise. "He wanted to help and I needed a hand with the locking drawer. How is the drop box working out?"

Paula waved good-bye to their last young visitor before she answered. "Thanks for coming." The little boy smiled shyly, then slipped his small mittened hand into his dad's big gloved one to go out.

"Just fine. It's easy to use," she said to Zach. She looked over at Norville, counting out cash and separating the bills into piles. "I know we did well tonight. I don't want to interrupt him right now, but he said something about taking in close to a thousand."

"That's great. Denver Dave did right by us."

"He really did. Which reminds me. I have to send him a thank-you note and a basket of treats."

"You never stop, do you?" Zach asked jokingly.

"The work doesn't, so I don't."

He nodded. "I think Edith has another project for me."

Paula laughed. "Be careful about saying yes to her. Unless you want to be working here until Christmas Eve."

"I honestly wouldn't mind." His deep blue eyes crinkled with a smile.

"Seriously? Didn't you say you did seasonal installations?"

"Finished 'em all by the end of November," Zach said. "Better yet, the checks are in the bank. So December is open for me. I could stick around."

That was the best news Paula had heard all week. But she kept her professional face on. Composed. In charge.

"What about your family and the ranch?" she asked.

"My older brother drove out last night," Zach said. "The way we work it out, it's officially his turn to oversee the place and help my parents, so I could stay in Denver, hang out at Jake's."

"Beats paying for a hotel around the holidays," Paula said.

"More or less what I was thinking."

Paula's head turned at the noisy clattering coming from the kitchen.

"Here we go again," Norville muttered.

He had the bills counted out and bundled and was stuffing them into a bank bag. Someone on the board had donated a small but sturdy safe to hold cash. The bag would go into it until tomorrow when the money could be deposited. He'd told Paula that a credit card reader had been ordered to process other transactions.

"Time to close down! Everyone go home!" Edith's trilling voice ended the conversation. She came through the swinging door, banging a large metal mixing bowl with a spoon. "Volunteers! Elves! Wrap it up and let's get out of here!"

"I think they can hear you," Paula said with a smile.

Edith took in the sight of Zach and Paula standing together and gave a pleased nod. But she was on a mission. "You too! Out!"

"Want me to get your coat?" Zach asked, moving toward the front closet.

"Not yet. I'm supposed to leave last," Paula said. "Insurance reasons. I'm in charge of security, at least for now. You can go if you want to."

He hesitated. "Mind if I leave with you?"

"Uh . . . no." She didn't want to look at him, didn't want to seem hopeful. But she felt Zach's intense gaze on her.

"We could go somewhere, get something to eat," he said.

"Sounds good. But no gingerbread."

"I'll call Jake. He knows every restaurant and bar in Denver."

With her coat and his jacket hung up on the diner's rack, they slid into the window booth, where place mats and cutlery were already set out. Outside of the red vinyl upholstery, which was permanent, nothing about the interior reminded Paula of the holidays.

"Good pick. Quiet place," she said. "And they don't seem to know it's Christmas."

The faint rattle of a spray can outside got her attention. Working fast, a bundled-up person on the other side of the window began to squiggle white foam letters onto the glass.

!SGNITEERG S'NOSAES & SYADILOH YPPAH

The background was filled in with foam dots for falling snow. The hand holding the spray can made wide sweeps over the bottom of the window to quickly create drifts, finishing the job.

Zach laughed as Paula put her head in her hands. "I take that back," she muttered.

The waitress came over with pad in hand. "Hello. Can I get you something to start?" she asked.

"Yes. Buffalo wings, please," Zach said.

"Coming up. That's our most popular appetizer. I think a fresh batch just came out of the fryer."

The waitress set down two glasses and two menus and left.

Zach perused his for all of three seconds. "I want the burger platter with everything."

"Starved, huh? You're working hard."

"It's fun. But I'm not pulling a double shift like you."

Paula acknowledged that fact with a weary nod. "Even so. If I eat too much, I won't be able to get up early. I'll just have a plain burger."

The buffalo wings arrived. "Here you go," the waitress said. "These are really hot."

They ordered their entrées and waited for the wings to cool. Zach leaned back against the red vinyl. "So here we are. It's nice to get you alone."

"We were hoping to be that busy," she said. "Careful what you wish for, right?"

"I noticed you're pretty good at crowd control."

"They covered that at the police academy," she said wryly.

"Mind if I ask why you became a cop?"

"Long story. I'll make it short. Have a wing." She nudged the appetizer platter toward him.

Zach took one and started in on it.

"I got in trouble in high school now and then. Never anything major but I got parked on a bench in the neighborhood police station more than once, waiting for my grandmother to pick me up after some idiotic stunt."

Zach looked at her quizzically.

"Like climbing the fence at the fair instead of paying, that kind of thing," she clarified. "I got assigned to a nice cop who took the time to talk with me. And she really listened. It helped. A lot."

"Got it. Interesting," Zach said.

"Anyway, I decided against a life of crime," Paula said lightly.

He nodded. "So is that why you keep an eye on Brandon?"

"Yes," she said after a pause. There was something a little less friendly in Zach's tone when he asked the question. "I appreciate you taking time with him."

"Seemed like the thing to do. He was just standing there watching me."

Paula looked at him levelly. "Do you have something you want to tell me about him? Just say it."

"Brandon seems like an okay kid. Those other two—"

"They ran away, whoever they are," she interrupted with a touch of impatience. "I haven't seen them since, have you?"

"No. But what I was about to say is that boys get into trouble differently than girls do."

"That's your opinion. Not mine. Nowadays they're about par."

"Okay. Maybe you know more than I do," he said calmly. "I can live with that."

She didn't smile.

Zach changed the subject. "By the way, I went up to the attic to see if I could find that window you were looking out of. The door was locked. Is that the one?"

Paula nodded, nibbling on a wing. "Edith turned it into a break room for the volunteers. I'll show it to you."

"I don't have to see it. I was just curious."

He polished off most of the platter and then their burgers came. Paula wasn't hungry, but she ate hers anyway.

Paula declined the waitress's offer of coffee. "None for me, thanks."

Zach said the same and asked for the check.

"On me," he said to Paula.

She didn't argue, getting up when the bill had been settled to leave with him. They'd come in separate vehicles but parked close together behind the diner.

She clicked open her car door with the remote tag on her keychain and got in, looking up at him as she slid behind the wheel. She said good-bye and was about to shut her door when he put a hand on it.

"Okay with you if I follow you home?" he asked. "It's late. Just want to make sure you get in safely."

For a moment Paula was taken aback. "That's not necessary," she said. "But thanks."

Zach gave a slight nod. "I'll head out to Jake's, then."

"Tell him I said hi."

He waited until her car had rolled out of the lot to start his pickup, then turned in the opposite direction, glancing once as she went around the corner.

He drove back to the Christmas House. The mansion loomed darkly over the sidewalk, shuttered and silent. The light at the top of the stairs illuminated the new sign.

Zach slowed down. He realized that the sign was swinging slightly, although it hung in a sheltered spot and the wind had long since died down. He leaned forward and peered through the windshield.

No one was by the front door. But it bothered him. He drove the pickup halfway around the block and turned off the headlights as he approached the empty parking lot.

He was just in time to witness two boys scramble over the fence and jump down into an area that was deeply shadowed. They landed on sneakered feet. The second one stumbled but the other yanked him away. They ran into the night, not making a sound.

No way in hell he could ID either one.

Zach stayed in his truck. He found the flashlight he kept handy and drove near enough to give the back entrance to the mansion a once-over, rolling down the window. He'd have to climb the locked gate himself to get any closer.

The heavy door was shut tight. No paint scrawls on the wall. The flashlight picked up the faint glitter of glass on the stairs. As far as he could see, the windows were all intact. But the double set of motion-sensor lights wasn't functioning. He moved the flashlight beam up. One bulb was cracked.

A well-aimed rock or a BB gun could have done that. More likely a rock, he thought. The running boys hadn't been carrying anything. Zach sat there with his foot on the brake. A steady dripping sound penetrated his thoughts. He used the flashlight again to find the source of it.

The cold snap had caused icicles to form above the housing for the lights. There were meltwater stains he hadn't noticed around the electrical connection. The motion sensors might've shorted out from the drip at some point and frozen again when the temperature dropped, cracking one bulb and blowing the other.

He'd let Paula do the detective work tomorrow. Zach doubted the boys would be back tonight.

Chapter 4

Paula brought her laptop with her the next day, going up to the attic room to run background checks using police databases. The new volunteers came up squeaky clean. They needed a replacement for Norville, who was going out of town for a week to visit relatives in Nevada. He'd promised to stay on until they found someone.

Still, she preferred a personal recommendation for anyone who handled cash. Records could be falsified and crimes covered up, especially if they were minor.

Paula heaved a sigh. The new people would have to be assigned to tree trimming and cleanup after closing time. She just wasn't comfortable with handing over a key to a box that held more than a thousand in cash each night. If necessary, she could pitch in at the door herself.

Fortunately, other basic security issues were covered for the moment—the broken motion-sensor lights had been replaced, for one thing, and the dripping icicles above them whacked away. Zach had told her what he'd seen in a matter-of-fact way without making any accusations.

Her cell phone chimed. Edith's number appeared on the screen. Paula picked up.

"Hi there. How are things on the first floor?" It was easier to use cell phones than to holler up and down the grand central staircase.

"I'm on the second," Edith puffed. "On my way up to see you."

"Stay there. I can come down," Paula offered.

"No. I need to talk to you in private."

"Oh. Okay."

Paula went to the door and opened it, looking out into the hall as Edith's blond head appeared at the bottom railing of the stairwell. The last few steps had the older woman breathing hard. She paused on the landing.

"That wasn't so hard last week," Edith grumbled. "You would think I'd be accustomed to the climb by now. I blame Christmas cookies."

"You could be right. Come on in." Paula followed her into the room. "I brought a bag of baby carrots."

"I'll have one. For medicinal purposes." Edith helped herself from the bag on the table and sat down heavily on the bed, nibbling on the carrot. "The postdinner rush starts in an hour. There are more people every day. We need a doorman."

"I'll put that on my list."

"Check with me before you assign anyone," Edith said absently. "I have someone in mind." She looked at the laptop. "What are you doing?"

"Standard background checks on the new volunteers."

Edith frowned, a look of concern in her eyes. "I guess you have to, with so many people coming and going around here."

"Everyone so far comes up clean," Paula reassured her. She sat down at the table and entered a password to get out of the databases. She put the laptop on standby, waiting a moment until the screen went dark. "So what's on your mind?"

Edith's frown changed to a faint, sad smile. "Brandon. Who else?"

"He's been good as gold around here," Paula said.

"I know," Edith replied. "But he's not always here. He was picked up yesterday evening at the high school for hanging out under the bleachers."

"That's not a crime. Not even a misdemeanor."

"The school was closed and the area's posted. No loitering. They let him off with a warning."

"Was he alone?"

"I didn't think to ask," Edith said thoughtfully. "I mean, he was by himself in the police station. But don't they keep troublemakers separated?"

"Yes. But I'm not sure if I would call what he did making trouble."

Edith gave her a mock glare. "Oh, don't make excuses for him. I do it too often myself."

"If they let him go, sounds like no one took it too seriously. Kid, you can go. Sign here. Scram."

"Were you there?" Edith asked. "That's exactly what the sergeant said."

"No. But I know how the station gets this time of year."

"I'm sorry. I shouldn't complain," Edith said. "You have enough to worry about on your day job."

"True enough," Paula conceded. "But I forget about it when I'm here. I'm having a great time. Thanks for making me volunteer. It keeps me from putting in overtime."

She'd taken on too many extra shifts this year, banking the money for a down payment on a little house in the Denver suburbs. Except that she'd never gone to look at any. But the nest egg was growing. Knowing it was there almost made it worth it to deal with crooks and crazies day in and day out.

Staying on the bed, Edith leaned back a little, bracing herself with one hand. "Someone had to drag you out of your apartment," she replied. "Of course, I benefited and so did the Christmas House, but a gorgeous girl like you has to have some fun. Speaking of that, I heard you and Zach Bennett left together last night."

"We did. In separate cars. We got something to eat and then we went home. In separate cars."

"It's a start," Edith said impishly.

"Think so?" The question was entirely rhetorical. Paula looked at her watch and got up. "Seven o'clock. I'm supposed to be downstairs."

Edith leaned all the way back onto the bed. "Tell everyone I'm resting. This bed is more comfortable than I thought."

Paula took her place at the entryway table next to Norville, who was sporting a loud red shirt with a green tie.

"Glad you could make it," he said. "I was getting lonely. Hey, before I forget, that Zach boy was just in here looking for you."

"Oh. What did he want?"

"He didn't say. But he's been tryin' to persuade me to play Santa for the big party. I told him I don't have the time or the tummy."

Paula smiled. Norville was definitely on the lean side. "There's room in that shirt for a pillow, and the party's not for ten days," she said. "I thought you were only going away for a week."

"Plans change. You have plenty of time to find someone else to ho-ho-ho. Fake beards make my chin itch."

She heard a muffled banging coming from the front doors and rose partway from her chair to see who was doing it. Several small hands were thumping on the glass. Parents pulled the children back.

"Edith's right. We do need a doorman," she said, rising from her seat and going around the table.

Brandon stepped up and doffed a top hat to her. He ran a hand through his black curls, obviously not used to the way an old-fashioned topper could flatten hair. His hazel eyes gleamed with amusement.

Paula opened her mouth in surprise, but he spoke first. "Good evening, Miss Lewis."

He put the hat back on his head at a jaunty angle and ran his white-gloved hands along the lapels of a dark, brass-buttoned overcoat. A candy-cane-striped muffler completed the look.

"What? Where did you—"

"My grandma said she doesn't want me standing around doing nothing. She rented this getup. I actually kind of like it."

"You look great." Paula admired him for a moment. Brandon seemed proud of the long coat and the glossy black top hat. The striped muffler was the perfect colorful touch. She gave it a tug. "Ready for the stampede?"

"Yup."

"Go for it."

Brandon strutted to the doors and flung them open.

"Happy holidays!" he called in a bright voice. "Line up, please!"

The restless children stopped for a moment to stare at him, then obeyed.

Paula caught a glimpse of the shy smile he received from a pretty brunette babysitter with dark doe eyes who seemed to be about his age. Brandon tipped the top hat to her and winked. The petite girl was as dazzled as if he'd been a rock star.

He straightened and stood tall. *Clothes make the man,* Paula thought. It was nice to see Brandon truly happy. And it didn't hurt that he had something to do that was all his own.

A flash behind her brightened the entryway. Paula turned to see Edith standing there with a digital camera.

"Just had to capture the moment," she whispered. "I

wasn't sure he would cooperate. He'd give me heck if he knew I was taking pictures."

She stepped back just as Zach entered from the hall, bumping into him.

"Oops, sorry," Edith murmured.

Bemused, Zach watched Edith scurry around him and away. The commotion at the front doors got his attention. He walked over to Paula. "What's going on?"

"Brandon is now our doorman," she said.

"How about that," he said in a low voice. "He looks like he's having a blast. I'm not sure I would want that job."

The two elementary-school boys with the babysitter made a beeline for the table. Other children and adults flowed past Brandon in an orderly fashion.

Paula ran back around to help Norville collect admissions. Zach followed her and picked up the stamp pad. "Settle down, kids," he said. "Everyone gets a star."

"I like the doorman," the babysitter said to Paula. There was a dreamy look in her eyes.

"That's Brandon Clayborne," Paula replied with a smile.

"I like his name."

Zach stamped the girl's hand. "Next, please."

The rest of the evening passed in a blur. A toddler had to be rescued when he escaped his mother's hold and climbed up on the fake fireplace with stocking puppets. One tug on a toe, and the row of stockings burst into song. The startled toddler burst into loud wails.

Once his tears were dried, he got over it—and turned out to be the last kid to leave, asleep on his dad's shoulder.

The volunteers were next, departing in groups of two and three, tired but happy. Edith brought up the rear. "Whew. Glad to go home," she said to Paula. "Don't stay too late."

"I won't," Paula promised. "I do a walkthrough when everyone's gone and that's it for me."

"We got the rooms pretty well cleaned up. Now, where is Brandon?" Edith called his name.

In a few minutes, the teenager appeared. He looked like himself again without the brass-buttoned coat and top hat. But there was a new authority in the way he walked.

"Here I am," he said to his grandmother.

"Did you hang up the doorman outfit?" she asked.

He nodded. "I know I have to take good care of it. I will."

Edith rolled her eyes for Paula's benefit. "Unlike the heap of clothes on his floor." She propelled him to the front closet to put away his rented duds and then they left. A few more volunteers straggled out.

But Paula knew she wasn't alone. She hadn't seen Zach go by. She quickly checked the reception room, the kitchen, and the rest of the first floor. He had to be up-stairs.

She listened, not hearing anything.

A walkthrough on the second floor revealed no one. She looked thoroughly, having once found a young child in a closed store and reunited her with her frantic family. Things like that happened. However, Zach Bennett would be impossible to miss.

Paula called up the stairs to the attic floor. "Zach? You there?"

"Yes," came the muted reply.

Sounded like he was in the small room. Up she went, wondering why he was there, although she could guess.

The door to the hall was open. She walked quietly to the room and hesitated on the threshold, looking at the big man silhouetted by the faint light from outside. Zach stood in front of the window, looking down into the parking lot.

"Keeping an eye on things?" she asked.

Zach turned to her with a smile. "Why not?"

She went to the window and stood beside him. A light dusting of snow brightened the asphalt below. Footprints made intersecting tracks to various cars. Some were idling and some were backing up to leave.

Brandon and his grandmother stood by the gate, waiting to enter as several vehicles drove slowly past them.

Paula saw him put his arm around his grandmother's shoulders and give her a brief hug.

"Aww," she said. "He really cares about her. It's not easy for either of them right now, but somehow Edith always manages."

She had the feeling that Zach had set aside his initial doubts about Brandon, but it didn't hurt to emphasize that he was a good kid.

"Where are his parents?" Zach asked. "You never did say."

"I don't think anyone knows. Even when he was little, he was with Edith most of the time."

"Maybe it was for the best."

Paula nodded. "I believe so. It's not something I talk about with Edith." She wasn't going to tell Zach that she'd first met Brandon when he'd been brought in to the police station.

She moved away from the window, looking at her laptop and making sure it was closed down before she disconnected the power cord. "I'm taking this home."

Zach cleared his throat. "Mind if I see you get there safely?"

Paula wound the power cord into a neat bundle. "Second time you've asked. I've never had a problem. I live in a safe neighborhood."

His gaze moved over her. She avoided it, not liking the glint of amusement in the depths of his eyes.

"Hey," he said easily. "It's just that where I come from, you get the girl to the porch and make sure the light's on inside before you say good night."

What a line, considering he carried around a snapshot of his girlfriend and had to know she'd seen it.

Paula gave a low laugh. "Oh. Is that all?" she teased.

Zach shifted his stance a little. His hands were jammed in the pockets of his jeans. Something had changed between them. The confined space of the small room intensified the heat that had risen through the house during the day. Unless it was his very male and inescapable presence that was making her feel so warm.

She slipped the laptop into its case and put it into her tote bag. When she straightened, he took a step forward. The slight smile he gave her was more sensual than amused. "Depends on the girl, I guess." His voice was husky.

Paula swallowed hard. "Okay."

Up here alone with Zach, suddenly without the constant distractions of a place filled with people and noise, all she could hear was the soft sound of his breath. She couldn't ignore how incredibly attractive he was. From the moment she'd seen his photo in the cruiser, she'd wanted him.

Too bad she knew there was a girlfriend. However, she hadn't confirmed that for a fact. Paula was a stickler for the facts.

Paula put down the tote bag and looked at him. "Well? I'm waiting."

Zach closed the distance between them and took her in his arms. His mouth was softer than it looked, covering hers and tasting her lips with an eagerness that made them part for his exploring tongue.

Her hand was crushed between them, resting over his thudding heart as he pressed himself to her. As his dark head rose, Paula gave a little moan, wanting more. Zach's warm breath stirred her hair as his fingers stroked through it, lifting the silken strands away from her neck. His hand moved down, gently rubbing her nape, then moved lower still to the small of her back. He pulled her top out of her jeans, caressing the bare skin. His touch was scorchingly sensual.

He brought her even more firmly against him as he captured another, hotter kiss, his mouth searching and urgent.

Paula arched her body, tilting her head back, letting her hair fall free. His lips lifted as he took advantage of the way she'd exposed herself, tracing kisses and skillful nips along the sensitive cord of her neck.

She was lost in his embrace, falling, yet held. He had her exactly where he wanted her. Doing exactly what she wanted him to do without a word being spoken.

There were no words for a kiss like this. It took all her strength to break away. Paula didn't dare look at the bed behind them. She stepped back.

Zach's hands fell to his sides. But his gaze still held her.

Chapter 5

Paula tried to compose herself, tucking her top back into her jeans. She couldn't look at him.

"That can't happen again," she muttered. "Not here, anyway." She got a hairbrush out of the tote bag and used the window as a mirror of sorts, turning her back to him. The lamp had never been switched on. The glass glowed darkly. She could barely see herself. She didn't want to.

Paula set the hairbrush on the windowsill.

Zach walked over and gently cupped her shoulders. The weight of his big hands soothed her nervousness but not for long. He pressed a kiss to the back of her head, then rested his chin on top of it. Keeping his gaze on hers in the dark window, he slipped his hands around her waist.

Paula removed them. "Stop it, cowboy. We went about as far as I'm going to go."

He took several steps back, allowing her to turn around without having to touch him. "Don't tell me you didn't like that."

She breathed sharply before she spoke. "I did. It's just that . . . this isn't the place."

And that he might be in a committed relationship and emotionally unavailable. She never allowed herself to be stupid for longer than five minutes if she could help it.

She held up a hand, fast. "And I'm driving home alone, before you ask. I don't think you're all that concerned with my safety."

Zach shook his head. "Not true, but have it your way."

"Thanks."

"What now?" he asked.

She picked up the tote bag, forgetting the hairbrush, and exited the room. "We leave."

He followed her down the hall to the top of the stairs, taking two steps for every four of hers. As Paula rested her hand on the banister, he put his over it. "Hold up. And sit down."

"Here?"

"Yes. I always thought stairs were a good place to talk."

She looked down the three flights, feeling a touch of dizziness. "Okay. You could be right about that." For one thing, she wouldn't have to look at him.

Paula sat on the topmost stair as he eased himself down beside her. She moved a few inches away and set the tote bag between them. The weight of the laptop made it *thunk* down.

"Can I make a suggestion?" he asked.

"Go ahead."

"Let's pretend that didn't happen."

"Won't work," Paula muttered. "It did."

"Okay. Here's another suggestion. We stay friends around here but we could, oh, go out on a date when we have the time. I think it would be a good idea to get to know each other a little better. Maybe we rushed things. But it was only a kiss."

A silent moment passed.

She didn't want to ask him about the snapshot she'd handed back to him.

"I really don't know what to do," she blurted out. "Every time you were around, I made sure I was busy—

too busy to think about anything like this. It wasn't exactly a strategy but it worked pretty well. Until now."

"You knew I was alone when you came up to the attic."

"Yeah. I'm a big girl. Like you say, it was only a kiss."

"Actually, it was two. Maybe two and a half kisses."

Zach rested his arms on his bent knees. His sleeves were rolled up to just below the elbows. She could see the muscles move when he clasped his hands.

"I don't want to read too much into it." She also didn't want to tell Zach that she'd never been kissed like that in her entire life.

"No," he agreed. "Me neither."

Paula stood up. "So is this conversation over?"

"Looks like it." He stood up too. Paula was annoyed that he seemed not in the least rattled. She covered by going down the stairs almost too quickly for Zach to keep up.

"Here we are," she said when she reached the first floor. Zach went to the closet, his long strides outpacing hers, and found her coat.

He held it out. She would have to turn around and slide her arms into the sleeves to put it on. Paula gave in. If he insisted on treating her like a lady, she might as well act like one.

She put the tote bag on the decorated table in the entry hall. He helped her into her coat. He seemed to be the soul of propriety. He could have been her married cousin from Missoula, except a whole lot handsomer. And not completely taken.

"You're all set," he said cheerfully. "Got the keys?"

He wasn't looking at her as he dragged his denim jacket off a hanger and reached high on the shelf for his Stetson. In a couple of swift shrugs, the jacket was on him, covering his broad shoulders and arms but open in front. He clapped the hat on his head, adjusting the brim to a slight angle by touch.

And then he stood there, his hands in the pockets of his jeans again. Looking way too sexy. Grinning like a cowboy who'd just gotten exactly what he wanted. Paula had only herself to blame.

"Yes," she said mechanically. "Would you mind holding the door open?"

"Not at all."

She walked past him, keys in her hand, and stopped outside. Zach came out and pulled the door closed. A police car came down the street and slowed. The window was rolled down by an officer she couldn't see, at the wheel next to his partner for the shift.

"Hey, Paula," he called. The voice, she knew. "We just went around the back. Looks good. Only a truck and your car in the lot."

"Okay." She held up the keys. "We're just locking up now."

"We'll be back," the officer said. "Every hour on the hour until dawn."

"Super. Thanks."

"Friends of yours?" Zach asked.

Paula nodded. "And colleagues, obviously. I asked the sergeant if we could get a patrol car to drive by more often. You heard what he said."

"Good idea." Zach looked after the police car as it drove away. "Does Edith know?"

"I mentioned it this afternoon. I'm not sure she was really listening. She seemed tired. She's here for the better part of the day and every evening."

"That's commitment," Zach said.

"She says it's plain crazy. I'm beginning to understand what she means."

"Then you need some time off," he said pleasantly.

"Like that's going to happen around the holidays," Paula scoffed. "Not for a cop." She went down the stairs, holding the wrought-iron railing and keeping her tote bag with the laptop in the other hand.

A little distance was what she needed right now.

They said good night once they were in the parking lot. Paula got into her car and left the window rolled up. She looked straight ahead as she exited, not at him, just in case he didn't get the idea.

If she ever had a free hour to herself again, she probably shouldn't spend it with a man who might have other commitments. One kiss—one fabulous kiss—still didn't change the fact that they were both going back to their ordinary lives when all the holiday hoopla was over and done with. Her in Denver. Him at the ranch.

The swing of high-set headlights made her glance at her rearview mirror. Zach was going the opposite way. She felt a twinge of regret when the pickup's taillights disappeared around a corner.

Paula snapped on the radio. She turned the volume down low, not listening to the music, and drove home to her apartment.

Her cell phone chimed with an incoming text before she got there. Paula pulled into her slot and put the car in park. She looked at the message on the screen. Zach.

Not sorry. That was amazing. See you in my dreams.

How romantic. What could she say to that? She settled for a straightforward reply, texting rapidly.

Let's stick with a date, Zach. What do you want to do?

His answer popped up quickly.

Ever been skiing?

She grinned and texted back.
Only in my dreams.

Zach's eyes looked even bluer in the brilliant sunlight bouncing off the snow at Winter Park. Ski goggles were shoved up over his forehead, making his tousled dark hair stand straight up. There was a ruddy glow to his skin from the fresh air.

"This is great," he said, looking around. "We were spending too much time indoors and working too late."

Paula frowned. "I still have to. Did I forget to tell you I just got put on the graveyard shift again?"

"I guess so. You slept all the way out here."

"Directives from on high. The sergeant has instructions from the brass to get the downtown drunks and rowdies under control after the bars let out."

Zach lifted the goggles and rubbed his forehead. "Who's riding with you?"

"I don't know yet. I'm not looking forward to it." She teetered slightly, then used the ski poles she was clutching to stand up straight again.

"At least you're here for the day. Just look at all that fresh powder. I can't believe you grew up in Denver and never learned how to ski."

An hour and a half to the west of Denver, the mountain scenery was breathtaking. She wasn't looking at it.

"Don't rub it in." She looked down at her rented skis. "So how do these work again? I can't seem to get the hang of it."

"You point the tips downhill," Zach said patiently. "Then bend your knees slightly. Hold the poles and tuck your arms in. Gravity will do the rest."

"I hate gravity. I already fell down five times."

Paula lifted the poles, flailed wildly, and collapsed.

Zach, to his credit, didn't laugh. But he had to be biting his tongue.

She just lay there. The soft snow was melting fast inside the padded collar of her down jacket. She should have worn something with a hood instead of the thick knit headband that looked so cute. Dimly, Paula remembered wanting to show off the auburn glory of her hair.

Zach towered over her, looking up into the limitless blue sky. "It's okay," she assured him. "I'm not hurt or anything. Thanks for asking."

"Come on." He reached over and hauled her up. "Try again."

"I'm afraid of the mountain."

"That's not a mountain. It's a mountainette. You can do it."

She stepped awkwardly in the skis, afraid to glide, hoping no one was watching. The only other skiers on the bunny slope were kids. They seemed to be having a great time.

Cautiously, she approached the three-foot-high mound of packed snow.

"Go for it," Zach called from where he was standing.

Paula took a deep breath and crouched slightly. Then she dug in her poles, pointed her skis downhill, and took off. To her amazement, she stayed up, gliding to a stop thirty feet away from the mound.

She whooped with joy and raised a pole to wave at Zach. Then she fell down again. But this time she didn't care.

Paula stuck with it. She stayed on the bunny slopes while Zach went off to do some real skiing. He patted her cheek with a massive glove and wished her well before he headed for the lift. She couldn't possibly see him in action, which was just as well. He looked too damn good in ski-wear.

There was just enough time for cocoa by the lodge fireplace when they were both done. Zach brought over the cups and two spoons and set them down on the low table.

"Feeling it yet?" he asked her. She shot him a puzzled look. "I'm talking about the aches and pains," he said.

"None so far. Maybe I'm just numb with cold."

He smiled. "It did you a lot of good to get out. You're really glowing."

"Sometimes I have to be dragged," Paula said. "Kicking and screaming."

Zach only shrugged. "All I heard was the word *yes*." His intent gaze warmed her more than the fire in front of them.

Paula plunked a spoon in her cup and stirred it for something to do. "The cocoa looks heavenly. Thanks." She took a sip. "Wow."

"Can't beat marshmallows and hot milk and chocolate for a flavor combo."

They sat back on the long, low couch. On a weekday at this hour, they had the lodge almost to themselves.

Paula got comfortable. They drank without saying much more, until Zach looked over at the clock near the bar. "Almost time to get you back to Denver," he said.

"Wish I didn't have to." Paula set down her cup and looked at him sideways. "It's so nice to just play and relax and do nothing. Not that I don't love my job."

"You don't have to love it all the time," Zach said. He rested a hand on his leg and stretched out the other along the back of the sofa. "Come on. Cuddle up. You're safe."

"From what?" She stayed where she was.

"Just come over here. This is the end of our first official date, and we are in a public area. Also, we have an audience. There are two little girls over there staring at us and hoping something interesting will happen. There is no way I'm going to kiss you."

Paula laughed and nestled against him. She curled up her legs and got even more comfortable. The little girls were led away by their mother, looking backward one last time to see Zach stroke her hair as she looked at the fire.

"How's that?" he asked softly.

Paula murmured with contentment and let it go at that. She didn't say the words that came to mind. *It feels wonderful. I want it to last.*

Chapter 6

The front door of the Christmas House had been left unlocked when Paula arrived the next day. It was early in the afternoon, too early for there to be many visitors. The volunteer who'd replaced Norville, a retired cop named Chuck Barbera whom she knew slightly, wasn't at the table. She walked into the empty front hall, unwinding the scarf around her neck—the weather had turned bitter cold.

No one seemed to be around, although she could hear the high voices of a few children upstairs. Paula set down her tote bag and looked at the box on the table. She lifted the lid. The slotted cash drawer was gone.

"Planning a heist?" Chuck's dry laugh made her turn around. "I got the money."

"Oh . . . good. For a second I didn't know what to think." She took off her coat and went back to the front closet to hang it up, keeping the scarf. The Christmas House felt drafty.

"Just seemed easier to take the drawer with me," Chuck explained, sliding it back in the box and resuming his station. "I was looking at the new installation upstairs. Things are slow."

"It might be a good idea to lock the front door if you or someone else isn't here," Paula pointed out.

"Edith gave me a bell for visitors to ring if I had to step away." He lifted a large metal bell and shook it vigorously.

Paula winced. "It's loud. But we could use a better system." She thought for a second. "We could do a webcam feed to a smartphone. Do you have one?"

"Yes."

"I'll look into setting something up. We can use a refurbed laptop. Just so long as it has a built-in camera."

"All right."

Paula tugged the sleeves of her sweater down to cover her wrists. "Brrr. Is there something the matter with the heat?"

"The boiler is acting up, now that you mention it. Edith said there's a man coming to look at it today. She went out to do some shopping."

That might mean an expensive repair. But they were doing well in terms of cash flow. "Good. Who's in today?"

Chuck slid the schedule toward her. She scanned the entry for the day, noting that Brandon was marked down for one to five. Paula's brow furrowed. Unless the high school was closing early, he shouldn't be here. It wasn't like Edith to cut him slack on school attendance.

"Where's Brandon?"

"That young man is upstairs in the Elf Shop. He brought a visitor with him."

"Oh?"

Paula looked more closely at the calendar. Next to Brandon's name was a penciled-in addition in tiny, faint handwriting. *Tabitha*. No last name.

There was no specific policy on volunteers bringing in other people. They needed one. Paula added that to her mental to-do list. The Christmas House staff had to be vetted.

"She seemed like a nice young lady," Chuck said. "About his age, I would guess."

"What I'm wondering is why they aren't in school," Paula replied.

"I asked him that. He said something about a teacher day, whatever that is."

Chuck and his wife didn't have kids, Paula knew. He might be easy to fool. She took her laptop out of her bag and got it going, typing quickly when the screen came to life. She entered the name of Brandon's school in the search bar and added *calendar*.

A pdf of a grid with the school's logo at the top downloaded slowly. Paula waited. Today's date showed nothing but a white square. She turned the laptop toward Chuck. "He was lying."

Chuck frowned. "Sorry to hear that. I took him at his word."

"It's okay," Paula said. "I'll go talk to him."

Paula stepped softly on the stairs. The Elf Shop was the first room off the landing. When she reached it, she heard a female voice, young and giggly.

Paula hesitated. Brandon really wasn't supposed to be here and she had no idea who Tabitha was. But they had put down their names in plain sight. And playing hooky wasn't a serious infraction. She didn't want to storm in and confront him.

At least he was here and surrounded by adults. She could keep an eye—or ear—on him until she found Edith.

She took the tote bag next door, into the room with the Twelve Days of Christmas display. The animated birds and animals and figures of lords and ladies were still and silent. There was no sense in having everything going at all times. The noise would be overwhelming. The young children she'd heard when she entered passed by the door and went down the stairs with whoever was looking after them. It was quiet again.

Paula unfolded a chair and a tiny table, and opened the

laptop to start looking up prices for refurbished laptops. The conversation in the next room drifted in.

"I don't want to do homework. Let's go on Facebook," Brandon said to his guest.

"Okay."

Paula heard keys click. So they had a laptop too. It must belong to the girl. Edith was planning to get Brandon one for Christmas.

"This one's cute. That was me last Halloween. Read my wall."

Brandon obliged. " 'My mommy and daddy went out to party,' " he said in a singsong imitation of her voice. " 'To-tall-y clueless. They're not allowed to friend me, because they keep saying they're not my friends—they're my parents.' "

He laughed. Paula's mouth drew down in a frown of disgust.

"I put on pointy ears and drew whiskers with eyebrow pencil and went as Tabby Cat. Do you want to know why I'm lapping up the milk in that cup?"

She didn't wait for Brandon to reply. Paula could guess the answer.

"I put a ton of Captain Spike's Coconutty Rum in it," the girl bragged. "I swiped it from my parents' liquor cabinet—they don't ever lock it. I loooove coconut rum."

Spoiled and unsupervised. Paula knew the type.

"Yeah? Cool. Me too."

"You're just saying that," the girl giggled.

"No, I really do like rum."

Paula happened to know that anything stronger than beer made Brandon throw up. Another bit of information that Edith had insisted on sharing.

"Can I call you Tabby? That's a good nickname."

The girl heaved an exaggerated sigh. "I guess so."

"What's your last name?" Brandon asked. "You never did tell me."

"Nyah, nyah. I don't have to," the girl answered. "Chat room rules."

So he didn't know her well and they had met online. The girl did sound as young as he was, maybe even younger. Paula wanted to get a glimpse of Tabitha, but she stayed where she was. Listening was one thing. Peeking through doors was another.

The two of them looked at more photos, alternately silly and serious. Paula was grateful she'd been a teenager before the Internet became a universal obsession. The photo of Tabby drinking and her snotty comments about her parents would live online forever.

But Paula had no idea what Brandon posted on Facebook and had never looked at his page. No teenager would want a cop to friend him, even though he was always polite to her.

"That's me, here at the Christmas House," Brandon said.

The girl yawned. "Who's the giant in the plaid shirt?"

"That's Zach Bennett. He's nice. He's teaching me some carpentry."

"Bang bang. Hammers and nails. Bor-ing."

Brandon dropped the subject. "Want to see my family?"

"Okay," she said with no real interest. "I don't have anything else to do until I meet my mom on Sixteenth Street. She thinks I went shopping on my own. Did I tell you that?"

"No. Okay, this is my grandma, Edith."

There was a pause. "Those earrings are weird. Looks like she got them at the dime store."

Paula waited for Brandon to say something in defense of his grandmother.

"Maybe she did," he finally replied. "But she's pretty cool."

"So, like, do you live with her?" the girl asked in the

same bored voice. "I don't see any photos of parent-type people. Just you and that old lady."

"I haven't seen my folks for a while."

"Oh. Why not?"

"Their choice. Not mine," he said evenly, his tone suddenly adult.

"You mean they abandoned you? That's really sad." The girl's sympathy sounded feigned.

"Not exactly. They just left."

"Like, recently? Right before Christmas? That's so mean."

Paula hated the way the girl was idly digging for information from a boy she didn't know and wasn't likely to see again.

"Years ago."

"You're lucky," Tabby said. "I wish my mom and dad would take a fast walk off a cliff sometimes."

Brandon didn't answer her. "But I have other family. Moving right along . . ." There was a clatter of keys. "This is my uncle's page. He's my father's brother."

"You look like him a little," Tabitha said.

"I look more like my dad."

"How come there's no photo of him?" she asked.

"There just isn't. Wait a sec. I want to read this." Brandon paused. "He says he just saw my dad in Vegas. Says he looked okay."

There was an undercurrent of excitement in his voice.

"Well, why didn't your uncle tell you?"

Brandon blew out a frustrated breath. "He doesn't even know I look at his page. He doesn't set controls. Anyone can view it."

The girl laughed. "What a dork. Wish we could add mustaches on everyone in his stupid photos. Then he'd know we were lurking. But not who we were."

"Yeah. Too bad we can't."

Brandon was pretending to be as bratty as Tabitha. Paula understood it, but she didn't like him for it.

The girl hummed. Paula imagined her looking around.

"We could get a marker and do it to the elves," she suggested.

"No."

"I brought a whole set." Paula heard the sound of scrabbling in some kind of bag. "Come on. What are you scared of? How would anyone know we did it?"

"Don't, Tabby."

The girl got to her feet. Paula heard Brandon do the same. The ring of an unfamiliar cell phone stopped them both.

"Oh please," said the girl. "It's my mom. Be quiet. I have to make up a lie about where I am. Even though she let me cut class to go shopping." The ringing stopped as Tabitha picked up. "Mom? Is that you? I can hardly hear you. I'm trying something on—what? Stop yelling. Are you there? God, I hate this crappy phone you bought me!"

She ended the call. "How was that?" she asked Brandon.

That was enough for Paula. She got up and went into the Elf Room. The two teenagers whirled in surprise.

"Hello, Brandon," Paula said. She looked at the girl, who was fair-haired and very thin, with heavily made-up eyes. "I don't think we've met."

"You're right. We haven't. Who are you?" Tabitha began.

Brandon hung his head. "That's Paula Lewis. She's a cop."

Tabitha glared at her. "What, undercover? She doesn't have a uniform."

"That doesn't matter," Brandon muttered.

"I didn't do anything!"

Paula ignored the girl's sneering hostility. "Can I see some ID, please?"

"Were you listening to us?" Tabitha snapped out the question.

"I heard some of what you said," Paula replied calmly. "And I am a police officer. Do you have a school ID or a driver's license?"

"I don't even have a permit," the girl said crossly.

"Let me guess. You're under sixteen. I'll settle for a school ID, then."

Angrily, Tabitha picked up an expensive leather back-pack and searched through it. She pulled out a laminated ID and thrust it at Paula.

"Thank you." Paula noted the locale of the high school, an upscale suburb north of Denver, and the girl's full name, Tabitha Emily Greene. "You're a long way from home. How did you get here?"

"My mom drove in and I walked over from Sixteenth Street."

"Got it. That matches up with the charade on the phone."

"But—"

"Don't talk back. You shouldn't be here and I'm not going to let you waltz out. Your mother doesn't know where you really are and you're underage. Call her and ask her to pick you up," Paula said firmly.

"I don't want to. You can't make me." Despite her bravado, Tabby suddenly sounded shaky.

"The other alternative is a ride to the station in a squad car and a chat with a detective from the juvenile department. Call your mom."

The girl gave in, speed-dialing her mother with a sullen expression.

Paula brought her and Brandon downstairs and asked Brandon to sit at the table. She waited with the girl in the entryway hall until she saw a luxury car pull up. The woman at the wheel rolled down her window and peered up at the sign for the Christmas House. Her anxious face brightened only a little when she saw her daughter push through the doors.

Paula turned away. Brandon looked at her, his mouth set in a tight line.

"Come with me," she said to him.

Chuck Barbera minded his own business. He had been a cop; he knew the drill.

The boy walked at her side as Paula headed to a small room off the kitchen. Its shelves were crammed with supplies, but the metal card table was stowed in there, along with a couple of chairs.

"Sit down."

"I guess you're going to tell my grandma."

Paula shook her head. "You get to do that. But make sure you tell her the truth."

Brandon nodded. He dug at a chip in the table's enamel paint, then stopped with a sigh. "Sometimes I wish you two weren't such good friends."

"That's not the point," Paula said. "Look, what just happened isn't the end of the world. But she had to go. And you shouldn't have brought her here in the first place."

"No. Sorry," he mumbled.

"Do I have to tell you that online hookups can be dangerous?"

Brandon's expression turned stubborn. "She's a girl. Not a homicidal maniac. Besides, I know someone at her school. He said she was fun."

"That's not exactly a character reference." Paula paused, trying to get a sense of what he was thinking. "You could do better," she said at last. "I can't say I liked her."

"Tabby seemed nice online. I didn't know she was so bitchy in person."

He'd still gone out of his way to try and impress her. Paula sighed. "Okay, so you made a mistake. I just don't want you making one that could come back to bite you."

He only shrugged.

"Listen up, Brandon. The Christmas House is for everybody. But it's not your house. You have an opportunity to help out, make some real friends, and maybe learn a few things."

He scowled. "What you're really saying is don't screw it up. Everybody keeps telling me that."

"I don't think I ever have."

He got up suddenly, jarring the table.

Paula pushed back her chair. "Where are you going?"

"Don't worry. I won't run away," he said sarcastically. "Zach needs help with the new display. He said he'd be here by three."

Paula looked at her watch. "That's a half hour from now. Go call your grandmother. Explain what happened. She can talk to me if she thinks it's necessary."

"What if I don't want you to talk to her?" the boy challenged her.

"Oh, come off it, Brandon. You did something dumb and it's over. I think we understand each other."

"Yeah. Maybe." He took the few steps to the closed door and opened it, looking into the hall to see if anyone was there. Then he swung the door wide, banging it into the wall, and made himself scarce.

Paula sat there, thinking for a few moments. He really hadn't done anything that bad. What worried her was the excitement in his voice when he'd seen his dad's name. She wondered if he would tell Edith that part.

Vegas wasn't that far away. All Brandon would have to do was hop on a long-distance bus to try and find him.

The dusk-to-dawn shift was weirder and more dreary than it ever had been, even from the relative security of a patrol car. On nights like this, Paula was a whole hell of a lot less sure why she'd ever thought being a cop was the be-all and end-all.

She was dedicated to doing her job right, and she gave it everything she had. But the thrill was kinda gone for Paula. For the last year or so, she'd had no time for her friends, who'd moved on with their lives anyway. That, and the ability to shut down emotionally—an occupational hazard for all cops—led her to expect the worst and see the bad in people too often.

A happy-go-lucky guy like Zach could help her change that. Plus he kissed like he meant it.

Still and all, a *little* caution was in order. It wasn't like he was guaranteed to stick around. That came with the cowboy mentality.

Though she liked the way he didn't seem to be weighed down by anything, even envied him that. Maybe it was his outdoorsy upbringing. City streets could eat you alive. Among other things, Paula knew she couldn't fix the people who called them home. These days, when she got back to her place at the end of a shift, she just wanted to curl up in a ball. That wasn't good. That needed to change.

She and her partner got out several times, scoping out different huddled groups on the sidewalks—homeless vets, the mentally ill, and older kids who she knew were runaways. They all had some version of a "family" on the streets and stuck with their own kind. The ones who wandered alone tended to be a lot worse off.

She and her partner persuaded some of the loners to go to shelters. Temperatures were dropping fast and space on the heating grates was something that got fought over. They broke up a battle that was turning nasty and called for backup to get a few of the slower-moving participants jailed for the night. The others took off into the night.

When the dust had settled and they filed their report, Paula slid into the passenger side and let her partner, Mike

Samson, a chunky, middle-aged cop who'd seen it all, do the driving.

"What a night. But it's a job. Nothing more, nothing less," he said philosophically. He looked over at her. "You all right?"

"I'm just tired," she said.

"That's because you try too hard. Do like me. I put in just enough effort so I don't get fired before I can retire."

Paula didn't answer.

"Want to drive over to the pretty part of town? We could issue a few drunk-and-disorderlies and call it a night. The ones in fancy clothes usually cooperate."

"Whatever."

"I detect a noticeable lack of enthusiasm," Mike said. "You used to be so gung ho."

"Not tonight."

"Maybe that volunteer gig is too much for you. I keep seeing those Christmas House flyers in the break room. Your face is in half the photos."

"Is it? Those must be the new ones."

"You look happy, though," Mike said.

Paula smiled slightly. "It's a happy place. I like it there."

"What do you do exactly?"

"I cover basic security. And I try to keep the peace. You know how it is. Always something."

"Yeah? Can't be that bad," Mike said. "Bet you wish you were there right now."

Paula looked ahead, getting her bearings. "We're not far away." Three rights on side streets and they would be at the Christmas House. "Turn here," she said. "I can show you what it looks like."

"Okay."

In a few minutes they were driving past the old mansion. A lamp somewhere on the first floor made the windows glow faintly from inside. The motion-sensor lights that illuminated the parking lot flashed on when they stopped for a moment.

"Looks nice," Mike said with approval. "I like the wreaths in the windows. Maybe I'll stop by with my wife and grandkids."

"Do that."

Paula settled back on the final go-around, watching the mansion in her side view mirror. She almost felt that she didn't want to let it out of her sight. For a fraction of a second, she saw the topmost window light up, as if someone had switched the lamp on and off quickly.

She turned around to look. The window was dark. It stayed dark.

"Something the matter?" Mike asked.

"I don't think so. Just thought I saw something. Could have been a reflection."

"Want to go back?"

Paula looked harder. Still nothing. "No. Maybe it was my imagination."

A cold dawn was breaking by the time she got home. Paula barely noticed the pink-and-gray sky as she went up the stairs to her apartment building and let herself in, collapsing in the armchair with her heavy uniform jacket and hat still on.

She rubbed her eyes, knocking off the hat. Paula picked it up and sailed it across the room. The equipment belt pressed uncomfortably into her middle. She unbuckled it and sat up to remove it, dropping pounds of gear and her gun onto the floor.

She sat back. Something was still poking her. Paula felt behind her and pulled out the TV remote. She clicked it on and closed her eyes. It was noon when she awoke.

Her cell phone was chiming. She looked blearily at the screen. Zach. Texting.

"Thank you for not expecting me to talk," she said aloud. She read the text.

Truck conked out. I bunked down at Christmas
House. Fun but lonely. Miss you. Coming in today?

Paula raised her eyebrows. So she hadn't been imagining things last night. She texted back.

Yes. Where are you now?

The reply came quickly.

About to knock on your door.

Chapter 7

Paula rushed over to the mirror and yanked the elastic from her tight but frizzled braid. Her hair had been under a police hat for eight hours and slept on for eight more. Rippled auburn strands fell around her pale face. She fluffed them up with both hands, then dashed on lip gloss and rubbed her cheeks for color.

The ugly uniform was staying on. There was no time to change. She could hear Zach in the hall.

There was the knock. "It's me," he called.

Paula went to open it, stumbling over her equipment belt and the items she'd removed from it. She picked up the belt and draped it over a chair.

"Hi," she said when she opened the door. "I look like hell. I slept in my clothes."

Zach laughed. "So did I. The boiler finally died around midnight."

"Again?"

"It was a challenge to keep warm." He walked in, looking around without sitting down.

"I'm surprised you didn't freeze," Paula said. "Want some coffee?"

"I can't stay long. But okay." He kept on his denim jacket, as if he were still cold.

"How'd you get here?"

"Chuck Barbera gave me a ride. I heard him opening up and I ran downstairs. Scared the daylights out of him."

"I bet you did."

He looked around her place with interest. "So this is where you live."

"All I do is work. This is where I sleep," Paula said. "Is the pickup still in the lot?"

"The tow truck came this morning. The guy at the garage just called, said it looks like a distributor wire shorted out. Should be ready by afternoon."

"Oh. Okay."

"Anyway, I got through the night. That house was built to withstand bad weather."

"You should have called me." She went into the kitchen and got busy with the coffee preparation.

"You were at work. It wasn't exactly an emergency."

"So tell me how it happened." The energizing smell of brewing coffee filled the small apartment.

Zach stood in the doorway of her small kitchen, bracing his arms against the sides. His jaw showed stubble that was lighter than his hair but not by much. It looked good on him.

"Chuck left me the keys and I did the walkthrough. I locked up and went into the parking lot. The truck was stone-cold dead and it was late, so I decided to go back, stay there, and not bother anyone."

"How was it with no one there but you? And what do you take in your coffee?"

"Sugar and milk."

She added both to his mug and handed it over.

Zach took a big sip. "This hits the spot. I'm still cold. If you really want to know, it was kinda fun and kinda creepy. Especially the new display. You don't want to be in the Land of a Thousand Santas with just a flashlight and all those twinkling eyes."

She still hadn't seen that installation. "Didn't they put a bed in there?" she asked. "I thought I saw the guys lugging one when I was at the front table."

"That was a padded sleigh," he informed her. "I tested it. I couldn't stretch my legs out, so I went up to the attic."

"Ohh. I did a drive-by with my partner after midnight," Paula said. "I saw the lamp up there. It was on for just a second or two."

"That was me," Zach said. "I had it on just long enough to put my phone where I could find it again and take off my boots. Then I jumped under the covers. Plenty of 'em. But I still couldn't get warm."

She was unsettled by the thought of him in the bed in the room where he had kissed her hard and well.

He finished his coffee and handed her the mug for a re-fill.

"You should have come up," he joked.

"Because I saw a light in the window? I had no idea it was you. I thought it was a reflection."

"Just kidding." He eased his muscular frame into a spindly kitchen chair that creaked under him. Zach turned his head to look at what he could see of the chair. "This needs fixing."

"It's always been like that," Paula said quickly. It was tough enough having to watch his hands when he did woodworking jobs at the Christmas House. He wasn't going to do it here. She changed the subject. "You sure it wasn't the thermostat? The boiler is ancient."

"Six of one, half dozen of the other. Eventually it came back on. But the radiators were banging."

"At least the pipes won't freeze."

"I don't think so." He leaned back, slouching comfortably but still sitting tall. "So let's talk. Sounds like Brandon got into a little trouble. He told me as much. He had a one-day suspension today."

Paula looked at him over the rim of her coffee mug. "I will never understand why schools punish cutting class with a day off. I guess you know what he did. And that he brought an unauthorized visitor to the Christmas House."

"He said she was pretty."

"Maybe so, in a way," Paula conceded. "But she was also spoiled rotten. And rude."

"He told me that too."

"Is he feeling guilty? Good," Paula said.

"He might be," Zach replied. "Then again, maybe not. I don't think teenagers know what the hell they're doing half the time. I didn't when I was that age."

She looked him over. He didn't seem inclined to fill her in on his wild past, if he'd had one. Paula let it go.

"I couldn't believe he got mixed up with someone like that," she said. "Miss Tabby Cat, as she calls herself, was a piece of work."

Zach nodded. "Apparently Brandon knew next to nothing about her."

"So I gathered. But it didn't stop him, did it? He'd better not try that again with some other girl, even a nice one. The House isn't his personal party pad."

"I think you got that across loud and clear," Zach said calmly.

Paula narrowed her eyes at him. "This is a switch. I used to feel like I had to defend him to you. Now it's the other way around."

Zach studied her for a long minute. "I honestly don't think you were that bothered by the girl or by him playing hooky. What's on your mind?"

Paula put her coffee mug in the sink and gave the faucet a swift turn to fill the mug with water. "Nothing worth talking about."

Zach got up and put his mug next to hers. "Maybe not today. But he'll be at the Christmas House after school tomorrow."

"He didn't happen to say anything about his dad, did he?" Paula asked. The question slipped out before she really thought about it.

"Nope. Edith did, though. But to Brandon, not me. She didn't know I was listening, not that I meant to."

"Me neither," Paula said.

" 'Don't you dare go looking for him' is what she said. From what you told me, I could figure out the rest. She sounded really angry."

He'd made a shrewd guess—or maybe Brandon had confided in Zach and sworn him to secrecy. Paula washed both mugs and turned them upside down in the dish drainer. "She was talking about his father. Count on it."

Zach shrugged his big shoulders. "Guess so. I try to stay out of other people's family quarrels." He chucked her under the chin when she turned around to face him. "And I think you should do the same."

Paula pushed his hand away. Random smooching didn't entitle him to hand out unsolicited advice. When it came right down to it, she'd never liked any kind of advice.

"I've known Brandon and Edith a lot longer than you have, Zach."

He gave her a long look that she couldn't really read. She couldn't tell if her action had bothered him.

"I understand."

"Do you?" She picked up a dishtowel and started wiping down counters that didn't need wiping.

He didn't say anything more on that subject. Paula stopped what she was doing and faced him with her hands on her hips.

"Zach, you'd better go. See you at the House, okay? I need to take a shower."

He didn't budge. She flicked the towel in his direction and he grabbed the corner of it. He used it to pull her to him when she wouldn't let go. His intense blue gaze moved over her face, stopping on her mouth for a second, then up to her eyes.

"Spare me the sexy stare," she said tightly.

He only smiled.

"Quit it. I can't think straight when you get too close to me." Paula dropped the towel. "And I don't want to play tug-of-war. Now go."

"In a minute. I have something for you."

"What?"

He slipped a hand into the inside pocket of his jacket and pulled out a square envelope made of cream-colored paper. "Your invitation to the benefit dance," he said as he handed it over. "The board of directors wants us volunteers to mingle with Denver society. I'd love to take you."

Paula shot him a wary look and opened the envelope without saying yes or no.

"The Grand Ballroom at the Miner Hotel? That's a historical landmark. I didn't even know it was open."

"It is. And recently restored to its former splendor," Zach informed her. "They rent out the main floor for events. But it's not operating as a hotel."

"Oh. We went there on a field trip when I was in elementary school," Paula said, forgetting her irritation. "I think I saw that ballroom. It had peeling red velvet wallpaper and giant moose heads. I remember the glass eyes. I thought they were looking at me."

"Maybe the décor has improved."

"Let's hope so." She looked at the invitation again. "Eight p.m. Next Saturday. I guess I have to be there."

"You didn't answer my question."

"I'm thinking about it. What's the dress code? It doesn't say."

Zach looked over the top of the invitation and pointed to the line that said *Frontier Formal*.

Paula made a wry face. "What does that mean?"

"Call Edith. If it's Western and it's historic, she's on it."

Paula rolled her eyes. "True enough."

"So will you go with me?"

Zach seemed about to smile again. He was so damn sure of himself. But that smile of his made her feel good all over, even when she wasn't in the best of moods. It wasn't his fault she'd slept sitting up. Paula gave in.

"Okay. I guess so."

"Excellent. Then it's a date. Our second. I'll polish my spurs."

Paula took a magnet from the fridge and stuck the invitation under it. "Don't get carried away, cowboy," she said. "I don't even own a dress."

Edith found that out soon enough. She'd bustled Paula out the door of the Christmas House to go buy one without letting her take off her coat.

Now here she was in a dressing room at Denver's finest department store, surrounded by dresses and long gowns, none of which fit right or looked good.

"How are you doing in there?" asked a cheerful sales associate on the other side of the door.

Clad in bra and panties and thick, baggy wool socks, Paula cracked open the half door. "Not too good. You can take all these back."

"Want me to bring more? I know your size by now."

It had been over an hour. "I don't know. What's left on the racks? I think I tried on everything."

"Oh, lots of things. Don't you worry. I'll look in the back."

Paula handed over the dresses, doing her best not to

drag the long gowns on the carpeted floor. "Sorry to waste your time."

"Not at all. My goodness, some of our customers take much longer than you and never buy anything."

The sales associate slung everything over her shoulder and clutched the hangers, trotting away.

Paula sat down on the tiny chair to await her return. She didn't look in the mirror.

She hadn't had the chance to dry and style her hair after her shower, and getting stuffed into a knit cap hadn't done much for it. It hung in damp waves around her face.

She dug in her purse for her cell phone for something to do. There was a text from Edith.

Find anything purty?

Paula put the phone back without replying. There was a rustling sound that made her look toward the door and then under it. A drift of gorgeous sparkly material was going by in the dressing room corridor.

"Isn't this fabulous?" someone outside said, apparently to a friend. "I wanted to get a look in the three-way mirror." Paula heard a whoosh as the woman twirled around. "Oh my God. I never saw anything so beautiful. I'm buying it. I don't care how much it costs."

"It's an investment," the friend said.

Paula was tempted to peek out. But no one had asked for her two cents.

"Do you think I can get heels to match?"

"If not, you could have satin ones dyed."

Paula hadn't even thought about high heels. She did have a couple of old pairs in her closet from her two stints as a bridesmaid. The silly dresses she'd given away to charity. She looked down at her baggy socks.

Frontier Formal. Maybe she could get away with cowboy boots, if she could find pretty ones. Of course, those would cost a fortune too.

A light rap on the door snapped her out of it. "Miss? I found a navy blue gown that would be nice with your auburn hair."

Paula's heart sank. "Ah . . . that's the color of my uniform. I'm a cop."

The sales associate seemed undaunted. "Really? I never would have guessed. It comes in other colors." Her feet stayed planted. She wasn't going away.

Paula opened the door and looked at the dress. The style was nice. "I'll try it on."

She took the dress and stepped back inside. Paula hung it up on a hook and looked it over. Cut low, it draped into curves, even on the hanger. She unfastened the side zipper and pulled the dress over her head, tugging it down over her hips. It fell into soft folds around her ankles and clung everywhere else.

Paula faced the mirror. She had never looked so glamorous. She looked at the price tag and gulped. No way. Not in navy.

The sales associate's feet were still on the other side of the door.

"What other colors does this come in?"

"Lime green. And wine."

Paula smoothed her hands over her hips and turned to look at herself from the side. The navy was elegant but it still reminded her of her uniform.

"I'll try the wine."

"Okay."

In another half hour, she was handing over a credit card at the register. It was a lot to spend for a dress she would wear for only one night, but as the other woman had said, it was an investment.

In what, Paula didn't know. But she needed a reason.

"Our shoe section is on this floor, you know," the sales associate said, handing over the charge slip for Paula to sign.

"Very convenient," Paula said, scribbling her name with a wild flourish. "I do need heels to match."

The sales associate boxed the dress in tissue and slipped it into one of the store's handsome shopping bags. Paula took the handles and heaved a sigh that was half happiness and half relief. That hadn't been so hard.

Chapter 8

Paula spent the early part of Saturday evening fussing with her hair to save the expense of going to a salon, figuring if she didn't like the results, she could soak her head, get out the hairdryer, and start over. But big rollers produced the waves she needed to experiment with a few different styles.

The classic wine-colored gown could be a turn-of-the-century look with the right hairdo and jewelry. Her grandma's jet necklace and earrings, which Hildy had inherited from her grandmother, would be perfect.

She gathered up her auburn hair and pinned it into a Gibson-girl knot on the top of her head. *Not bad,* she thought. The updo certainly showed off her neck. Then she pulled out the hairpins and let the waves tumble over her bare shoulders.

The look would suit a frontier bad girl, but she liked it. Zach was sure to. Ultimately, Paula decided on a combination of the two styles: a soft knot with a few strands left free.

She did her eye makeup first, not all that sure of herself. But she had time. Mascara and liner worked magic. She grinned at herself, pleased with the sultry look she achieved.

Paula went to get the dress. Just slipping into something

so expensive and well made was a sensual pleasure. She padded barefoot to her dresser, enjoying the way the material rustled faintly over the floor.

The box with the antique jet jewelry was in the top drawer. She brought it back to the mirror. Once her hair was up, she put on the necklace, something she had never worn. The sparkling beads were fashioned in a complex design, finished with a jet pendant that rested just above her cleavage.

The effect of the delicate black necklace against her creamy skin was startlingly sexy. The ladies of long ago definitely understood the art of allure.

Earrings next. The long drops trembled when she tossed her head.

Paula adjusted the bodice of the gown, revealing more of her shoulders, and turned sideways to gaze into the mirror. It was nice to be a woman for a change and not a buttoned-up cop. She batted her eyelashes at herself and almost laughed out loud.

If Grandma Hildy could see her now, she'd be amazed. Paula had always been a tomboy. But dressing like this was seriously fun.

She glanced at the clock. Zach would be here soon. It was time to practice walking in high heels. She looked at the floor of her apartment. Between her clothes and her cop gear, there was an obstacle course.

Paula slipped on the wine-colored high heels, another extravagance, and swanned around. Wonder of wonders, the shoes didn't pinch and didn't make her walk funny.

Her cell phone rang. Paula grabbed it.

"You ready?" Zach's warm voice did something to her.

"Yes."

"Then I'm coming up."

She picked up the clothes and other things on the floor in record time, stuffing it all into her bedroom closet just as he knocked on the door. Paula took a deep breath. She snuck one last look at herself in the mirror, then went to answer the door.

Zach's eyes widened as he took her in from head to toe. Then he whistled. "Wow. You look fantastic."

"So do you."

Zach was dressed like a gentleman rancher of yesteryear. He wore a fitted black twill coat with notched lapels and a gray silk vest. Tailored black trousers broke perfectly over polished boots with engraved silver tips. His strong jaw was freshly shaved, set off by a high-collared white shirt with a flat black tie that crossed at the ends. All that thick, dark hair of his was more than long enough for a frontiersman.

She touched a fingertip to each of the shirt's pearl studs and stopped at his tie.

"But I'm not sure a gentleman should whistle at a lady," Paula said primly. She toyed with the ends of the tie.

"My apologies, Miss Lewis. I meant no offense." He captured her hand and pressed his lips to it. The sensation was delicious. His steady gaze became slightly hooded as he looked down at her, struggling to keep his eyes on her face and not her half-bared bosom.

She heaved a sigh just to torture him. "You are forgiven. You look extraordinarily handsome tonight, Mr. Bennett. Please come in."

"Thanks." He strode in, taking the time to admire her from all sides. Paula twirled in the beautiful dress, making it flutter around her ankles. "Maybe we should skip the ball."

"Absolutely not," she said indignantly. "This dress cost a fortune."

"Whatever you spent, it was worth it," he laughed. He preened a little himself. "Like my outfit?"

"I do. Where did you get it?"

"Doesn't matter. No one's going to notice what I have on. Not with you on my arm."

"I don't know about that. Let me get my coat." Paula went to the closet by the apartment door and picked out a dark coat instead of her everyday one. It would have to do.

Zach took it from her and draped it over her shoulders. "You don't have to put this on all the way. I'm right out front."

"Great. That's easier."

Long black velvet evening gloves were next to a black beaded purse resting on the table. Her makeup, a comb and hairpins, and her credit cards and ID were already in it. Carefully, she drew on the long gloves, smoothing the soft velvet over her hands and clasping them demurely.

Zach drank in the sight and nodded with very male approval. "Covering up could be better than getting undressed."

"Mind your manners, sir," she said with mock disapproval as she picked up the small purse. But she knew exactly what he meant. Then he stepped to the door, back in his gentlemanly mode.

"Allow me." He opened the door with a flourish and a bow, straightening just as she swept by him. Paula turned to lock it and walked down the hall, enjoying the unfamiliar click of her high heels on the floor.

They were still inside the building's front foyer when she stopped to look out through the glass. There was a limousine at the curb. A uniformed driver spotted Zach behind her and sprang to attention, opening the back door and standing ramrod straight by it.

"Is that—" She turned to him, her eyes wide.

Zach grinned. "It's ours for the night. Couldn't get a horse and carriage. Sorry about that."

She stood on tiptoe to kiss his cheek. "You're wonderful."

"I try." He moved to the outer door to open it for her.

The coat over her shoulders wasn't enough to ward off the intense cold. Zach took her arm, guiding her down the short flight of stairs to the limo.

Paula got in, not all that gracefully, unused to maneuvering in a long, full dress. "Last time I did this was my prom." She sat back and scooted over, making room for Zach by gathering up the folds of material.

He sat back and stretched out his long legs. "Same here. This is great. Kind of makes me wonder why I don't do things like this more often." He looked over at her. "I can answer that. Because I never had someone like you to do it for."

"Aww." Paula didn't mind the outrageous sweet talk. It went with his costume.

The driver closed the door and went around to his side. A sliding window separated the front seat from the capacious banquette in back.

"Ready to roll?" the man asked, glancing back at them.

"Yes, thanks," Zach replied.

The driver slid the window closed and moved the limo away from the curb.

Paula looked out at the uncrowded streets. The tinted windows of the limo gave the city a faintly unreal look. Holiday lights strung on lampposts and handsome old buildings added to the effect.

She turned to Zach when he moved closer and slid his arm over the back of the seat.

"This is magical," she whispered.

"Glad you like it." He pressed a chaste kiss to her temple. "I still can't get over how gorgeous you look. It's going to be hard to restrain myself until we get to the Miner."

She nestled closer. "I don't want to walk in looking all rumpled."

"People might talk," he murmured.

They drove on. Paula was blissfully happy right where she was, but she looked up at Zach. "Let them," she whispered.

He bent his head to hers.

The driver had to circle when they reached the landmark hotel. There was no space long enough for the limo, and double-parked vehicles blocked the curb. Women in long, Victorian-style gowns and evening coats were going up the wide exterior stairs on the arms of their escorts. Some of the men were dressed like Zach, but none were as dashing.

"Just drop us up there," Zach advised the driver, then turned to Paula. "It's a little bit of a walk. Is that okay with you?"

"Yes," she replied. "I don't want to make a grand entrance, thank you very much."

The driver pulled over some distance ahead. "I'll call you when we're ready to leave," Zach told him.

"Yes, sir. That will be fine." The man got out and went around the limo.

"You rented this for the whole night?" Paula asked.

"Of course. I had no intention of driving you in the pickup. Which is fixed, by the way. So how late can you stay out, Cinderella?"

He bent his legs and moved toward the door. Paula followed his lead, gathering up the folds of her dress to keep from getting tangled. "I have to work tomorrow."

A frown of disappointment crossed his face but only for a second. "Oh."

"Don't look at me like that. I had to sign up for extra hours to make up for missing a late Saturday shift."

"Can't be helped," he said, his voice almost curt. "If we have one night, let's make the most of it."

He swung himself out and up when the driver opened

the door. "If you can find a spot outside around ten, we'll probably be leaving then," Zach said to him.

Paula got out with his assistance, looking down the street at the stream of arriving guests. She let Zach drape her coat over her shoulders again, shivering a little in the icy night air.

He looked down at her with a twinkle in his eye. "Better fix your lipstick."

Paula looked in her purse for her compact mirror and saw to that before they headed for the hotel.

Once inside, she let him check her coat. Paula stood in the restored lobby, looking around at the gilt-encrusted splendor of it all. The flocked red wallpaper gave the space warmth.

Just beyond immense old doors garlanded with Christmas greenery was the ballroom. There had to be a hundred or more guests inside. Several men cast curious glances her way, taking her in from head to toe just as Zach had.

He rejoined her, slipping the claim ticket into the watch pocket of his gray vest. "You are the belle of the ball."

Paula shook her head. "I doubt that." But she slipped her gloved hand through his arm and faked a confident air.

They went into the ballroom, hearing murmurs of admiration on both sides. Zach was an imposing presence, even though he was one of the few younger men there.

"That outfit gets attention. The women are staring," she whispered out of the side of her mouth.

"I only have eyes for you," he replied in a low voice.

"Good," she said. "Is there anyone here we know?"

"There's Brandon."

The boy was weaving through the crush of people to get to them. "Hi, Zach. Hi, Paula. You look really pretty."

The respectful compliment touched her. "Thanks."

Brandon wore a dark suit that was a little too large for his slight frame. But his black hair was carefully combed, and Paula suspected he'd shaved off the peach fuzz. His face looked perfectly smooth.

"You clean up good, kid," Zach teased him.

Brandon pulled a face and jammed his hands into the pockets of his jacket. "My grandma dragged this out of the back of the closet. It's too big."

Now that he mentioned it, Paula noticed the hasty alterations to shorten the sleeves. "You wear it well," she told him.

The boy shrugged. "Gram said it used to belong to my dad. She keeps too much stuff."

"So did you bring a date?" Zach asked, breaking the moment of awkward silence.

"Nope. There's no one here my age either."

"Maybe later," Paula said encouragingly.

Brandon looked toward the dais, where a band of country musicians in old-timey attire were tuning their instruments and connecting amps. "I'm gonna go watch them set up, okay?"

"You bet. See you around." Zach looked back at Paula after Brandon walked away, a rueful expression on his face. "I wouldn't be fifteen again for a million bucks."

"I know what you mean. Sitting out dances, thinking no one likes you. I don't know how I survived it."

"Well, my momma taught me to two-step and waltz. That's about all the dancing I do. I'm hoping those guys play one or the other."

Paula stepped lightly away on his arm. "Personally, I would call myself a survivor of the classes at Mrs. Neugebauer's Academy. But not a dancer. Go slow. Be gentle with me."

He patted her gloved wrist. "Certainly, my dear."

They mingled for a while, since there was no music yet. Paula turned at the sound of a cheerful voice she knew well.

"Yoo-hoo! Paula!" A plume of feathers was coming their way.

Edith wriggled through the crowd, dolled up in a saloon madam's lavish gown. She held up her billowing skirts, apologizing to the amused guests for her bustle, which seemed to have a life of its own.

"Oh my! Don't you two look nice," she said breathlessly. "Can you believe I'm wearing a corset? If I eat so much as a cracker, I might just swoon."

"I believe that was the idea back in the day," Paula laughed.

Edith unfolded the fan she wore dangling from her cinched waist and fanned herself vigorously. The feathers in her piled-up hair bobbed. "Oh. Then I'll eat a whole pack. And if you see any gallant men who look like millionaires, send 'em to me."

She stopped fanning to inspect every detail of Zach's attire, brushing a bit of imaginary lint from his black sleeve.

"I declare, you are a good-lookin' man," she said. "Quite possibly the handsomest man in Denver. I'm going to tell all the other ladies that you are taken. You're dancing with Paula and that's that."

"Yes, ma'am," Zach replied with enthusiasm.

Edith spotted someone else she knew and began to move on, then turned her head. "But save one for me," she said to him.

As more guests entered the ballroom, the press of people grew.

"Want to get some air?" Zach asked.

Paula nodded.

With his arm around her bare shoulders, he guided and protected her simultaneously. They reached the side of the ballroom, where he pulled out a chair and took two flutes of champagne from a passing waiter holding a tray.

"So what is the plan for tonight?" he asked Paula.

"It's not meant to be all that formal, really. It's a meet and greet. Some speeches, some music."

Zach sipped his champagne. "I vote for more of the latter and less of the former."

An amiable-looking older man went up the steps to the dais and took the microphone. He launched into a rambling introduction of the ball's sponsors, looking through reading glasses at the paper in his hand.

By silent mutual agreement, Paula and Zach finished their champagne and sneaked out a side door.

"Too much hot air for me," she said with a smile. Paula took off her gloves and carried them as they walked down a long hall lined with sepia photographs of the hotel and its famous guests.

They stopped to look at a long-ago dignitary sporting enormous muttonchops and a handlebar mustache.

"Now that's what I call whiskers," Zach said, impressed.

"Don't you dare grow anything like that on your face," Paula teased.

"Okay. That leaves the top of my head. I could get his look with a can of pomade and a curry brush."

She reached up and lightly ruffled his hair. "I like you the way you are."

Her hand drifted down to caress his cheek. Zach's gaze turned suddenly tender. "Do you?"

She brushed a fingertip over his mouth. "Yes."

"Let's find someplace a little more private, Miss Lewis."

"This is a hotel."

He smiled down at her. "They don't rent rooms. What's on your mind?" he murmured.

Paula lifted her head, feeling utterly womanly and flirtatious. "Can't you guess?"

He pulled her into an alcove draped with curtains where no one who happened to pass by would see them, though they were alone. Then he took full advantage of her willingness. His arms encircled her as he began to kiss her, gently at first, then with passion.

She closed her eyes, yielding to him. The gloves she was holding dropped to the carpet without her knowing it. Zach's mouth claimed hers with a strength that barely concealed his need.

He tasted her lips, teasing them open with his tongue, moving his hands around her waist, caressing her into breathless acquiescence before his hold turned to iron and kept her firmly in place. Motionless, every tiny sensation she felt was that much more intense. She couldn't have stepped back if she'd wanted to—and she didn't want to.

Zach's eyes held a dark blue fire in their depths when he lifted his head. She licked her parted lips. He made a husky sound in his throat as he watched her. But he didn't kiss her again.

He turned his attention to her neck, pushing aside the jet drops in her ears, kissing, nipping but not hard enough to mark her skin. She wanted to cry out with pleasure but didn't. Zach let her go for a moment. It didn't matter. He might as well have bound her with silken rope. His hands caressed her shoulders, moving over the elaborate necklace, touching the jet pendant that dangled from it

With sure hands, he reached around to unclasp it. Zach slipped the necklace into his pocket.

Paula felt a chill but not because she was cold. It was the sensation of being bared to him that made her shiver. She sighed deeply and he held her by the waist again, lifting her and holding her against the wall with ease. His kisses moved from her neck to her collarbone, and lower still, to the swelling softness of her hidden breasts.

Paula sank her hands into his thick hair. She was literally in midair, being made love to fully clothed, with as much passion as if she'd been naked in his bed.

He let her down inch by inch. Zach's breath came raggedly. His eyes were shadowed with lust. There was no other word for it.

"How in the hell are we going to go back into that ball-room and pretend this never happened?" he growled.

Paula forced herself to answer. She tried to make light of it. "The same way we got out," she said. "Through the door."

Chapter 9

He pulled the heavy curtain back. They looked both ways before they stepped out of the alcove.

The band struck up a lively reel with fiddles, banjos, and a plunking bass as Paula and Zach went back down the hall. She had smoothed her dress. He had fixed his tie. They looked straight ahead. But they were hand in hand.

"That was interesting," he said.

She couldn't tell if he was joking or not. He couldn't be. He'd kissed her like his life depended on it. But maybe he was the kind of guy who always kissed that way. She still didn't know who that girl in the photo was.

Zach squeezed her hand when she didn't reply. "Maybe insane would be a better word. Or incredible. I liked it. A lot."

"So did I." Her response was more hesitant.

"Couldn't stop. Didn't want to. You just look so damn tempting in that old-fashioned dress, Paula."

She was silent.

"Perfect lady. Brazen hussy. Everything I ever wanted in a woman."

Paula could sense when he was looking at her. She avoided his gaze.

"We should time-travel more often," he added.

"I think we should get back to reality."

Now that it was over, the spectacular kiss seemed more like a moment of madness. It needed thinking about. But she squelched the analytical little voice in her head that demanded a comparative study and a list of possible consequences.

The hubbub from the crowd of guests echoed in the corridor. "Hold up," she said, stopping. "Do I look all right? Not too . . . kissed?"

"If you don't want people to talk, don't disappear for too long," Zach advised her. "How about we go back in for just a bit and then leave for good, go to your place and finish what we started."

"Not so fast. We need to talk first."

"Why?"

She wasn't totally swept away. "You're not spending the night, Zach."

"You're kidding."

Her gallant gentleman had been replaced by a cocky cowboy. "No. I'm not kidding. I'm not ready for that."

"My mistake." He gave her that slow smile.

Paula almost relented. Then she pictured the pretty girl in the snow and stiffened her spine. "Excuse me. You don't seem to be listening."

"Are you mad at me?"

"I'm getting there. Shut up, okay? It won't kill you." Paula had just realized she was missing something. "My gloves—shoot. I dropped them in the alcove."

"We can get them later. I'm not going back in the ballroom solo," he said. "Please don't storm out. I'm sorry for whatever it is you think I didn't do or should be doing right now, even though you won't tell me what that is."

"Look, there's Edith," she said, not wanting to pursue the conversation.

"And she's made a friend." Zach motioned toward the ballroom.

The crowd had opened up to make a circle for dancing. Feathers bobbing, Edith was kicking up her heels with an elderly gentleman who didn't miss a beat.

"Brandon must be dying of embarrassment," Paula said.

"Maybe not. I don't see him anywhere."

The reel speeded up and more dancers joined in, providing enough of a distraction to embolden her. The conversation would stay within bounds if they were with other people.

"Now's our chance. No one's looking. Let's go in," she said.

They moved to the nearest table with two chairs. Another waiter walked by with filled flutes of champagne. Zach handed one to Paula and took another for himself. They clinked their glasses like casual acquaintances, as if they hadn't just been lost in each other's arms and fought about it like fools afterward.

The wild reel got wilder.

Finally it ended and the dancers stumbled to a panting halt, laughing as the musicians caught their breath. The master fiddler held his violin and bow in one hand as he stood in front of the microphone.

He whipped out a bandanna to mop his forehead. "Whew," he said theatrically. "Ladies and gentlemen, we'll play a waltz next and take it easy on you."

Murmurs of approval rippled through the ballroom.

"I can't hear you."

Roars—weak roars—of approval followed.

"That's more like it," the fiddler said with satisfaction. "Now please pick up those pens you'll find on your tables and make your tax-deductible donations and pledges to the Christmas House."

A flurry of questions.

"That's right, in the white envelopes with a picture of the House," the fiddler said. "Checks or credit. This is their first year of funding programs for children in need all over the Denver metro area. Your help can make a difference. Thank you. We'll be back in five."

Zach set down his champagne flute. "When they return, Miss Lewis, if you would be so kind—"

She'd calmed down just a little. It helped to remember why they were here in the first place.

"I would be honored to dance with you, Mr. Bennett."

A nice, sedate waltz actually sounded good. One hand on his shoulder, one hand clasped in his. Twelve inches apart at all times. *Stick to the box step,* she told herself. And Mrs. Neugebauer never allowed her students to whirl. No looking into Zachary Bennett's deep blue eyes. Thank God there were no lifts in the standard waltz.

"There you are!" Edith whooped.

This time she reached them with ease, since so many people chose to sit down or wander off to look for refreshments. She snagged a chair from another table on the way, dragging it behind her.

"I saw you leave," the older woman said in a conspiratorial whisper that carried to the nearby tables. She sat down, catching her breath.

"We saw you dancing," Zach replied quickly. "Who was that man? Do I have to fight him for your honor?"

Edith laughed. "I might have to fight his wife. Just kidding." She peered at Paula. "You look different. Now why is that?"

Paula felt her cheeks color. "It's warm in here."

"No, that's not it." The older woman stared at her. "Oh, your necklace is missing. I hope you didn't lose it, honey."

"The clasp came undone." Zach pulled the glittering black strands from his pocket and handed the necklace to Paula.

Paula held it in her lap. "Thanks. I almost forgot you had it."

Edith looked at her and then Zach. "I know a good jeweler you can take it to."

Paula smiled. "That's okay. I think I can fix it myself."

"Suit yourself. You two aren't leaving again, I hope." Edith fanned herself. Paula shook her head no.

"I need you to stay here and chat with folks, glad-hand on behalf of the Christmas House, that sort of thing. I know you'd rather have fun and it's work but someone has to do it."

"Not a problem," Zach said after a fractional pause.

"We made out like bandits," Edith told them when the ball was over and they were waiting to leave outside the Miner Hotel. "The Christmas House board might be able to make an offer for the mansion."

"Do you really think so?" Paula asked.

Edith's eyes twinkled over the collar of the white faux-fur wrap she was bundled up in. "Some of the checks were very, very generous. Apparently several wealthy donors have visited the House incognito. They were impressed."

"You never told me that," Paula protested.

"I didn't know who they were myself until tonight. A couple of them stopped at your table to chat."

Zach looked at Paula.

"When was that exactly?" she asked Edith. "I got a little giddy for a while."

"Oh, you're always level-headed," the older woman replied. "Maybe too much so. Being giddy would be good for you."

Paula didn't know about that. "Did I miss anything else?"

"Oh—I almost forgot. The Denver police chief stopped by with the socialite he dates. He was on his way to another benefit but he'd heard about this one. I don't suppose you know him personally?"

Paula cringed. "No. I don't."

"He's a pretty good dancer. Ask me how I know." Edith

looked at both of them. Neither did. "Of course, I was hoping you would chat with him but—"

"Sounds like he had a great time," Zach interrupted. "It was a very enjoyable evening."

The old lady turned to him. "Yes. For one and all."

That was true in ways Edith hadn't guessed at. But Paula was exhausted. She'd managed to dance with Zach and not lose her head, and she made small talk with people she didn't remember and nibbled on hors d'oeuvres and champagne and now she had a headache.

They shouldn't have gone back into the ballroom. Uncertainty about the best kiss of her entire life had ruined the evening.

She pulled on her black velvet gloves. She'd retrieved them from the alcove just before their departure. Zach had called their driver, who'd said he was on his way.

The older woman peered into the darkness. "I wish Brandon would hurry."

"When did he get a learner's permit?" Paula asked.

"Just yesterday. He's about to turn sixteen, you know. The car's parked a block away but I get nervous. Especially because I'm supposed to be in there with him." She quailed under Paula's stern look. "Don't blame him. I promise never to do that again. Oh, here he is."

A small car drove toward them on the other side of the street. Brandon stopped and got out, looking pleased with himself.

His grandmother patted his cheek when he crossed the street and handed her the ignition key. "Well done," she said. "You'll have your license in no time."

Zach waved the limo over as soon as he saw it. The driver eased into a spot at the hotel's curb, pulling up in front of the four of them.

"Sorry, Mr. Bennett," he said. "I think there's something

wrong with the engine. I'd like to look at it before we leave."

"Sure. I'd help you but I can't get my hands dirty."

Brandon seemed surprised to see the limo. "A stretch? Way to go, man." The remark was addressed to Zach.

"I'm not rich," Zach said. "I just rent."

"Hi, Brandon," Paula said. "Congratulations on getting your permit." She wasn't going to be tactless and ask him if he'd enjoyed himself tonight. He'd been a good sport about showing up. She could skip the dumb questions.

"Thanks." He walked with his grandmother to her car, the suit jacket that had belonged to his father flapping against his narrow chest. He took the jacket off before he got in, bunching it up into a ball and throwing it in the backseat.

The Claybornes drove off.

"He doesn't look too happy," Paula said to Zach.

"Let it go. Live your own life. You can't fix what's bothering him."

The seriousness of Zach's tone got her attention. "Do you know something I don't?"

"He and I talked about a few things just before I came over to give you the invitation."

Paula had guessed right. She was relieved to be distracted from her thoughts. The excitement of hearing even a bit of news about his father must have ebbed away, especially if nothing had come of it. But Zach wasn't offering any details.

"It's good that he can open up to someone."

"I guess so," Zach said. "I don't think I can really help him. But if he wants to tag around after me at the Christmas House, I can find work for him."

"That counts as help in my book."

The driver straightened from under the hood, scrubbing at his hands with a rag. "I can't figure out why it's stalling," he called to Zach. "But I think we can make it as far as the lady's place. Unless you want to go to your friend's apartment first."

"Just a minute. We haven't figured that out," Zach called back. He looked hopefully at Paula.

"I have," she said in a low voice. "You aren't coming up. Just forget it and forget that kiss too. We still have to work together."

"True."

"Go to Jake's apartment."

"I will."

He didn't seem inclined to argue. That didn't sit right with her either. Would he go to Jake's, or somewhere he could find the satisfaction she wouldn't give him?

She made a cup of peppermint tea, letting the bag steep as she took off the dress and hung it up carefully. It was after midnight and she had to be at the station by eight on Sunday. Paula set her phone alarm for six-thirty and tucked it in the pocket of her terry robe. Swathed in its warmth, she went back into the kitchen, coming out with the cup and curling up in the pink armchair.

Paula was past thinking. What a night. She looked around her place. It was far from being a love nest. In fact, she'd never brought anyone here after a date. It was tidy most of the time; that was about all she could say for it.

There was no art to look at on the walls or homey knickknacks just for fun. The furniture was basic, bought for eating and sleeping and occasionally turning on a TV she barely watched. The overstuffed pink armchair was about the only piece that had personality. She had no time and no inclination for decorating.

She could write a book on the hazards of working too much and living alone. The trouble was she wouldn't want to read it.

Paula sipped her tea and set down the cup on the floor when she was finished, burrowing into the armchair.

When she woke up, the room was filled with rays of sun. Her phone alarm was chiming, louder and louder. Stiffly, she extended her legs, letting the feeling come back into them. Her bare toes touched one of the wine-colored high heels she'd kicked off.

Paula pushed herself up out of the armchair and took the phone from her pocket, shutting off the alarm. Her routine never varied. Shower, dry and braid her hair, put on her uniform and shoes and heavy jacket, and get out.

She was at the station ahead of time for roll call. Paula took a detour through the cubicle area, greeting a few of her colleagues who'd moved up from the rank and file to their own little low-walled forts. A few heads lifted as she walked by. Whether they'd partied last night or policed the streets, they all had that weary Sunday-morning look.

Levi Sarton, a friend from her academy days, jerked his thumb toward the sergeant's office. "He wants to see you."

Paula looked toward the closed door, debating whether to stop by her locker first or just go in.

"Get it over with," Levi added.

She was running through the possibilities in her mind. Had she and Zach had been spotted making out? Was there security-camera footage from the scene?

Zach Bennett, a cowboy and a gentleman, lifting her up. Nuzzling her cleavage. Kissing and more kissing. Police Officer Paula Lewis enjoying every second of it. The city blogs would have a field day.

"Okay, okay." She took off her jacket and hat and strode to the door, knocking on it. "It's me, Paula Lewis," she called.

"Come in," a gruff voice commanded.

The sergeant, a large man with beetling gray eyebrows

and a crew cut, looked sternly at her as she crossed the threshold. Paula quailed inwardly as she stood in front of his desk.

"You wanted to see me, Sergeant Meltzer?" She didn't quite meet his eyes.

"Relax," he barked. "It's good news."

Her knees wobbled inside her uniform pants. "Oh."

"Sit down."

Paula did, wondering what on earth was going on.

Sergeant Meltzer folded his huge hands on the desk. "Had a call from the chief first thing this morning. Said he heard about your work at the Christmas House."

She waited for the sergeant to say something about the benefit ball. He didn't.

"Oh. Yes," she answered vaguely. "I volunteer there between shifts."

"Yeah? When do you find time to sleep?"

"Real police officers never sleep, sir."

"Ha-ha. That's my joke. You can't use it." He picked up a pencil and tapped his desk blotter. "Anyway, he said to give you a paid day off today."

Paula's eyes opened wide. "Excuse me?"

"I said, loud and clear, you have the day off." Sergeant Meltzer's gray eyebrows went up as his voice got even louder.

"Yes, sir. Thank you." Paula stood again, bundling up her jacket. "And thank the chief for me if you talk to him again."

"Get out of here. And enjoy yourself." He pointed the pencil at her. "That's an order."

Paula drove home and changed. The day was clear and sunny, although it was freezing. She couldn't think of what to do with a whole day to herself. Although—for the first time—she didn't feel like spending it at the Christmas

House. They wouldn't be expecting her until much later, during the evening rush of families doing weekend things together.

She'd leave it at that. The thought of Zach entered her mind. She dismissed it. He and Jake would probably throw together a guy-style enormous breakfast and watch sports.

It would be fun to stroll around the shops on 16th Street and not be walking the beat. She could window-shop and check out the decorations, maybe get some coffee and a sandwich. That seemed like enough of a plan for now.

A half hour later, she was walking down the wide thoroughfare. Bare trees glittered with a touch of frost, their limbs and twigs outlined with fairy lights that weren't on during the day. But she could imagine it.

Paula just walked. Her unbraided hair was kept under control by a knit cap with a pompon on top, but some still brushed against her rosy cheeks. The strong wind barreling in from the Front Range got stronger as it blew through the buildings facing each other along the street.

She almost didn't hear her cell phone ring at first, then reached into her pocket for it, looking at the number. Edith.

"Hello," she said happily. "Guess what? I have the day off."

"Hey. That's great." The voice that replied was a boy's.

"Brandon?" she asked.

"Yeah."

"Is your grandmother all right?"

"Yeah. She's still asleep."

"Oh. Well, nice to hear from you. What's up?" Paula hoped Brandon hadn't wrecked the car. She didn't hear sirens in the background, which was reassuring. An unexpected call from a teenager wasn't usually good news.

"Um, I wanted to ask you something."

"Sure. Go ahead." Paula stopped in front of a shop window display of four-poster dog beds. Not something she needed but fun to look at.

He dropped his voice to a whisper. "I want to get a Christmas present for my grandma and I don't know what to buy. You know her pretty well. Any ideas?"

Paula smiled. "I'd have to think. Actually, I'm downtown right now."

"Oh, okay."

"I got a surprise day off," she added.

"Cool. So maybe . . . could I meet you?"

Paula was taken aback. "Sure. Leave a note for your grandmother, though. I don't want Edith worrying."

"I'll tell her I'm meeting Grace."

"Who?" It wasn't any of Paula's business but she asked anyway.

"Grace Finn. She's the babysitter who came in with those two little boys? The night I first worked as a door-man?"

The face of the pretty girl who had asked for Brandon's name came back to Paula. She had seemed so sweet. And responsible. She'd managed those kids just fine. She was Brandon's age too.

"Yes. I do," Paula said warmly.

"Well, she looked me up online. So we, uh, got together last week. Just to hang out. My grandma likes her."

"That's great. So leave a note. But don't lie."

"I'm not," Brandon said defensively. "I'm just leaving out the part about you. Me and Grace are going to meet near downtown later today."

"All right." Paula named a time and an intersection where she would wait for him, and went into a cozy-looking place for a scone and coffee.

He was at the meeting place on the dot, engulfed by a heavy parka with a hoodie inside it.

Paula saw him first. "Hi, Brandon," she teased, lifting the hood a little. "Are you in there? I can barely see you."

His loopy grin made her laugh. Whatever his problems were lately, he was still just a kid.

"Yeah. I'm way too hot," he said.

"My car isn't far away. You could leave the parka in it and we could go to an indoor mall."

He agreed. It wasn't long before they were exploring the first level of a pleasant shopping space that wasn't crowded with Sunday shoppers yet. He didn't see anything he liked and neither did Paula.

They rode the escalator up to the second level. Paula spotted a girl she recognized on the down escalator as it moved by them before she remembered her name. Fair hair, thin, heavy eye makeup.

Oh yes. She remembered.

Tabitha Greene ignored both of them, her narrow nose in the air. Paula looked at Brandon, worried that he would be upset. He only shrugged.

Easy come, easy go. Paula breathed a sigh of relief as they got off, deciding not to mention it.

"There are more jewelry stores up here," she said to Brandon. "One or two ought to have something she'd like."

"I'm just glad you're with me," he replied.

They browsed the windows, comparing items and trying to get a peek at the tiny price tags, which were turned to the blank sides.

"How about that one?" Brandon asked. "She loves that color."

He was pointing to a turquoise turtle pendant set in silver and strung on a silver chain.

"That's really nice. Bet she'd love that."

Tactfully, she didn't make a guess as to the price. Paula knew Brandon worked odd jobs occasionally, depending on his grades and getting Edith's permission. If the turtle was too expensive, Paula would make up the difference. Her friend didn't have to know.

"Let's go in," Brandon said, opening the door and holding it for her. He seemed to have already made up his mind. They went to the counter and he made eye contact with the sales associate, a blond woman with a stylish angled haircut.

"Could I see the turtle pendant in the window?" he asked.

Not *we*, but *I*. Brandon was quite the man all of a sudden. Even his voice sounded more grown-up. Paula was proud of him.

"Of course," the sales associate said, going for the keys to the back of the display. "That's a contemporary Native American piece. Beautifully carved, isn't it?"

"Yes. I like it a lot. And I think my grandmother would love it," Brandon said.

"Ah. I was wondering. But you"—she glanced at Paula with discreet curiosity—"are too young to be his mother."

"I'm a family friend."

She went to the window and unlocked the sliding glass, reaching carefully around other pieces to lift the turtle in its box. She brought it back to the counter and removed the turtle, showing it to Brandon with the full length of the chain draped over her hand.

"An old story says that the turtle is a symbol of longevity and patience," she said. Paula was amused by the woman's soft sell, which worked like a charm with men of all ages.

Brandon smiled. "That's my grandma all over." He let the woman place the turtle in his palm and looked it over, front and back. "This is real turquoise," he said. "It has different colors in it."

"We don't carry the chemically altered kind," the sales

associate said. "And the chain and the setting are solid sterling silver."

Paula knew without a doubt that the sale had been made. Now came the hard part.

"How much is it?" Brandon asked.

The blond woman turned the box over. "One hundred and fifty dollars with the chain."

"I'll take it."

Paula felt obliged to at least look at the pendant herself. "Before it's wrapped, can I hold it?" she asked Brandon. He handed her the pendant.

It really was a beautiful piece of jewelry and certainly something Edith would cherish. Paula gave it back to the woman, who busied herself with returning it to the box.

"Can you afford to spend that much?" Paula whispered to Brandon. She knew the sales associate could hear her, but she had to ask.

"Yeah." He pulled neatly folded twenties out of the front pocket of his jeans.

Paula hesitated. Okay. That looked like a fair amount of cash. He could have been saving for a while or earned it recently somehow. She controlled her curiosity. The money was his and the gift was for his grandmother.

He turned to the woman behind the counter. "What kind of gift wrap do you have?"

She brought out a small sample book. Brandon selected a turquoise paper that was the same color as the turtle. With swift sureness, the woman wrapped the gift and tucked a tiny card and stick-on bow to match in the shopping bag she handed to Brandon.

"I'm sure your grandmother will love it," she said. "Thanks for coming in."

They exited. Brandon looked happy, until a couple of teenage boys coming their way caught sight of the little bag and snickered as they went past.

He flushed. "The hell with them," he told Paula.

"I could fit the bag in my purse," she offered. "Just until we get to the car. Don't worry. I won't forget to give it to you."

He seemed relieved as he handed it over. "Okay. Thanks."

Paula looked up at the huge clock above the second-level promenade. "When are you meeting Grace?" she asked. "And where?"

"Shoot. I almost forgot. Can you drop me off at the corner?" He named the intersection.

"No problem."

"And, Paula—maybe you'd better hang on to the turtle until Christmas Eve. You know how grandmas are. They get into everything."

"I know exactly what you mean," she laughed.

Chapter 10

The standoff didn't seem worth it. Zach hadn't called her. She hadn't called him. Paula had stopped by the Christmas House late in the day on Sunday and he hadn't showed.

Monday and Tuesday came and went. Same deal. Paula knew she was making herself crazy checking her cell phone so often. Just in case . . . but nobody called. She bit the bullet and turned it off Wednesday morning.

Edith had asked her to lend a hand today. If his Royal Cowboyness showed up to do the same thing, Paula would be polite to him.

She picked out a sweater that just happened to be a deep, rich wine color. Other than that, the baggy fit and scrunched turtleneck wouldn't remind him of what he was missing.

She peered into the mirror. Her face looked pale and her eyes not there. Paula looked for the beaded bag that she'd taken to the ball. Her makeup was still in it.

For morale, she told herself as she applied a touch or two. Not for him.

She grabbed her coat and out she went.

The Christmas House was a hive of activity as she came through the front doors.

"Norville! You're back," she said happily as she hung up her things.

"Yep."

The older man didn't look her way. He was busy counting bills and sorting them by denomination.

"Did you miss us?"

"Nope."

"Well, I'm happy to see you. We're making money."

"Looks like." He finally glanced up at her, keeping a hand on the stack of bundled twenties. "But we may come up a bit short this week. Me and Chuck are counting the torn tickets and comparing them to the cash and credit card receipts." He didn't seem overly concerned as he added, "Tally's off. Not by much."

She was more interested in his other offhand comment. "Chuck stayed on? That's great. An experienced volunteer is worth his weight in gold by this point."

Norville nodded. "Didn't have to train him."

"I want to thank him. Where is he?"

"Right here. Hi, Paula."

She could barely see the retired cop behind the large plastic reindeer he was carrying, legs out. It looked like a lawn ornament, the kind that didn't light up. Paula dodged the hooves.

Chuck set the reindeer down and straightened an antler. "We were keeping the tickets in Rudolf here." He lifted the saddle for her to look inside. A heap of colored tickets filled the belly.

"You have to count all those? Gosh, that's a lot of work."

He looked at her hopefully.

"Can't," she said with no regret whatsoever. "Edith has a million things for me to do upstairs."

"Like what?" Chuck wanted to know.

"Ah . . . the toy drive committee has a meeting scheduled. She wants to use the folding tables and put a center-piece on each."

"Edith and her dang centerpieces," Norville muttered. "She used to do them for all our church suppers. She just can't stand a bare-naked table."

It was true. Paula laughed but Chuck Barbera didn't.

"She's going to show me all the tricks of the trade," Paula continued. "It will take a while and then I have to—"

"The girl's no fool," Norville interrupted. "Now sit back down, Chuck, and let's do this again."

Paula took the chance to make a rapid exit, heading for the stairs and knocking into a placard on a small easel.

Memories That Matter! Your Child's Photo with Santa! Today Only!

She straightened the placard. That ought to be interesting. There was no line yet but there would be.

She stopped at the storage room and dragged out the folding table inside, snapping the legs into the corners to lug it upstairs.

"Need help with that?" Chuck called.

Paula felt a little guilty at the question. But he had meant it sincerely.

"No. Thanks, though." Paula lifted it easily. "It's not that heavy. Just a little awkward."

She got it up to the second-floor landing and looked around, not remembering which room would be used for the toy drive committee. Then she heard Edith's voice.

"Candy canes, fake holly, snowflake placemats, battery-operated candles—check, check, check. Got everything."

Paula waited for someone to reply. When no one did, she realized Edith was reading from a list, to herself.

She went toward the half-open door and used the edge of the table to push it open. Just as she'd thought, Edith was alone in the Elf Room, standing amid several bags crammed with holiday goods. The other folding tables hadn't been set up and were leaning against a wall.

"Hi."

"There you are." Edith waved the list in her hand at the shopping bags. "Look at all these decorations. I cleaned out the dollar store," she said proudly.

"I see that," Paula replied. "Want me to start unfolding tables?"

"If you would. Just give me one so I can unload."

Paula brought over the table she'd carried up and unfolded it. She hoisted the bags up onto it and went to unfold the others.

"Where do you want the tables?" she asked Edith.

"Oh, not too close together," the older woman said absently. "There are folding chairs behind the door."

She had the first centerpiece completed by the time Paula was done. Edith carried it over and plunked it down. "What do you think?"

"Very cheerful. I like it."

The thing was definitely fun to look at. When the battery-operated candle was switched on, it would brighten up the plain table.

Edith went around it, shoving in the unfolded chairs with a hip and slapping down snowflake placemats. She stepped back to admire her handiwork.

"There. Winter enchantment."

Booted feet were coming up the stairs, providing a low drumbeat to high-pitched conversation. "Just in time," Paula said. "Here comes the committee."

"I'm ready," Edith replied. "Are you staying for this, honey?"

"No. I think I'll take a peek at the Santa photo session. The little kids usually show up now."

Edith found her purse before the committee members reached the door. "Take my camera and grab a few snaps," she said, holding it out.

"Thanks."

"We have a preschool group scheduled first. No mommies and daddies, just a teacher and whoever helps her. The families should start coming in after that."

"Who's our Santa?" Paula asked.

"Hello, Louise!" Edith didn't answer, distracted by the arrival of one of her best friends. "And here's Darla too! Come in, come in!"

Paula murmured words of welcome and edged out through the door.

"You can sling your coats on the back of the chairs," she heard Edith say. "There's just not much room around here anymore."

"That's how it should be," Louise replied. "Busy is best."

Paula went to the stair rail and looked down. She could see the parquet of the first floor and bright hats and hoods belonging to the preschoolers in puffy jackets.

"Are we ready?" a teacher asked the kids.

There were mumbled yeses, a few noes, and some coughs and sneezes. Santa would be lucky to escape without catching the sniffles himself.

"Then let's go."

Paula positioned herself in a discreet spot to record the event. She turned the flash off first. Santa was a big deal to these little ones. She didn't want to startle them on their way in.

Lumbering footsteps in the hall behind her made her turn. Santa was entering his domain from the small room set aside for dressing. He was older, by her guess—he walked slowly and stiffly, maybe because he was a huge guy and very heavy. That couldn't be all pillows around his middle. The snowy beard he wore almost covered his face.

Built for comfort. It was a job requirement.

The young teacher who'd organized the preschoolers

was almost at the second floor, with a young child on either side of her.

"Hands on the banisters," she said without turning her head.

A couple of aides relayed her words and made sure the children complied. Another aide brought up the rear of the colorful parade.

Paula leaned over the railing and took a few shots from above. Quickly, she checked the screen of the digital camera. Couldn't be cuter.

She welcomed the group and pointed the way to the room. No doubt the hired Santa had an assistant or two of his own—Edith always saw to things like that. And she had to have hired a photographer who was good with children to record the great moment for each one.

Paula wondered whether the Santa was a volunteer or a pro. Either way, everything should go smoothly enough.

She went down the stairs past the line of wide-eyed children, smiling. A few smiled back, but most were serious, thinking about what they would tell the old man with the big white beard when they got there.

The kitchen was emitting the wonderful fragrance of fresh-baked butter cookies. Paula decided to make herself useful by wrapping them up for sale and helping to eat a few of the broken ones.

It was another hour before she went upstairs again to see how Santa was faring.

The line was inside the room by now. Some small, satisfied customers were already outside sitting on their puffy jackets, supervised by the teacher and an aide.

Paula waved at them and peeked into the room. The back of Santa's thronelike chair was to her, but she could see the white pompon on his red fur hat move when he nodded. He rumbled a few words she couldn't quite hear and a *ho-ho-ho* as the child on his knee slid off and scrambled to join the others.

The photographer, a young man with an expensive SLR digital camera, crouched to get in position for the next shot.

There were only a few children left in line. Santa did his thing for each one, and the session concluded.

Arms folded over her chest, Paula watched the last preschooler scurry by, followed by the two other aides. She kept quiet. The photographer and Santa were conferring about something. The huge man stretched out one leg and then the other, rotating his heavy boots in circles and groaning under his breath.

"More work than you thought, right? You should get up and stretch," the photographer advised. "I'm going to go out and get some coffee before the next session. Want anything?"

The wearer of the red fur hat slumped down in the thronelike chair. The white pompon swung from side to side as Santa shook his weary head.

"Take a nap, then." The photographer put the camera next to his other gear and reached for his down jacket. "Back in a flash. Get it? A flash."

Santa groaned again, loudly. Paula felt sorry for him.

The photographer went past her in a hurry, giving her an instant once-over and a practiced smile that said he liked what he saw. "Hey there, beautiful."

She wasn't in the mood for dumb jokes or a lame come-on like that. Paula only nodded in reply, hoping he wouldn't try to ask her out later. He left, clattering down the stairs.

Santa sat forward, rubbing his temples as if he had a headache. Paula moved forward to ask. She could find him some aspirin if he did.

"Are you okay?" she asked. "I could get you some water or a soda."

He put a huge, gloved hand on his beard and tugged it off. Then he turned to her, brushing bits of white fluffy stuff from his handsome face.

"Zach?"

He pushed himself up to a standing position using the arms of the chair, wobbling in the heavy boots.

"Yeah. Nice to see you. I assume you don't want to sit on my lap."

"Very funny." She looked him up and down. "What on earth happened to you?"

"Got wrecked. And no, I wasn't drunk. The other driver was. He spun out in front of a semi and forced my truck into a guardrail. Not a scratch on him."

"When did that happen?"

"About a day ago, I guess. His car was totaled and so was my pickup. I'm okay, more or less. Just banged up."

Paula took in that information. "So that's why you were walking like that."

He looked down at the clumsy boots. "I borrowed these from a buddy of Jake's. I needed some extra big ones to go over the flexible casts. My ankles swelled up. Jammed, not broken."

"Zach, for heaven's sake—" She stopped, wanting to put her arms around him. But not if it would hurt.

"If you really want to know, I was thinking about you when it happened. I missed you. Then, *boom*. Hardly knew what had happened until a highway patrolman was asking me a bunch of questions. I was in shock, I guess. Then all I could think was that I wanted to see you even more."

He was rambling, but his recollections were sort of flattering. She hoped some of what he'd just said was true. And thank God no one had been seriously hurt.

"Did Jake bring you here?"

"Yeah. Late this morning. I slept upstairs for a while."

"You didn't have to come in."

He shrugged. A few of the pillows under his red fur coat slipped out. Zach didn't bother to pick them up. "I figured I'd be sitting and besides, I'd promised. Edith had the suit and that was that. I didn't tell her about the wreck and she didn't see me come in. So here I am."

"Yes, well . . ." Paula didn't know what to say or do. She looked around the room while Zach ventured a cautious stretch. "Do you have an assistant?"

"No."

"I'm volunteering."

He started to smile as he straightened. Then he winced. "Okay. I need one."

Paula slid her arm under Zach's and helped him back into his chair.

"This is crazy," she said, standing in front of him. He bent his knees carefully and got as comfortable as he could.

"I'll manage."

She put her hands on her hips. "Why didn't you call me?"

"They kept me in the hospital for observation. My phone died."

"Did you at least call your parents?"

"I did," he said. "My mother drove down from the ranch to take a look at me for herself. She agreed with the doctors that I was okay and drove back. I had a habit of falling out of trees when I was a kid."

"Which obviously did something to your brain. You could have asked Jake to contact me."

"I just didn't," Zach said irritably. "So stop yapping at me. My ears are ringing. Everything hurts." His gaze moved over her. "Except looking at you."

Chapter 11

The Christmas House closed to the public an hour later. Most of the volunteers had gone home by the time Zach tried to sneak past Edith, unsuccessfully. She extracted the whole story from him in less than five minutes and blocked his way.

"You're going straight to the hospital, young man."

"Been there." Zach slid up the white cuff of his red fur coat and showed her the paper-strip ID around his wrist. "Got the bracelet."

"I can't believe they discharged you," Edith fretted. "You can hardly walk."

Zach reached out and put a hand on the stair rail to steady himself. "They told me I would feel worse before I felt better. That seems to be true. But I can still put one foot in front of the other."

Paula put herself into the conversation. "Everything's under control, Edith. Really."

"I still don't understand why he even came in," she replied. "And you and I spoke on the phone this morning," she scolded Zach. "Not one hint of this did I get."

"I wanted to be here. I thought the kids would cheer me up," he replied. "And you know what? They did."

"Oh my Lord. When I think of those adorable children

climbing all over our suffering Santa . . . You are a hero, Zachary Bennett. A wounded hero."

Paula suppressed a smile. That was over the top, even for Edith. But Paula thought better of him for keeping his promise and making little kids happy. Even if it was stupid of Zach to drag himself here when he should be resting.

There was a knock on the glass doors. Edith turned around. "That's Brandon." She went to unlock the doors.

Zach smirked at Paula. "How come you don't say things like that to me?"

Paula gave him a level look. "Edith beat me to it."

He grinned as if he didn't believe that excuse for a second.

"Gram, just let me talk to him." Brandon had come in and was walking quickly across the floor toward them. "Wow. You look like crap," he said to Zach.

Teenage tact. Nothing like it, Paula thought. But Zach didn't seem offended.

"The truck looks worse," he said.

"Totaled? That's major, dude. What can I do to help? I could be, like, your driver until you get better."

Edith squawked and Zach flinched. "No," he said. "You just got your learner's permit."

It took another half hour before Paula persuaded Edith to let them go. The older woman got a promise out of Zach before she would even unlock the front door.

"I won't come in tomorrow," Zach said. "You have my word."

He got a grip on the iron railing and began slowly descending the mansion's front stairs.

Paula watched, shaking her head. He was managing without her assistance. But she wasn't letting him take a step more than he had to once he got to the sidewalk. She turned to Brandon and tossed him her keys. "Can you bring my car around to the front?"

"Sure."

"Thanks, kid." Zach had stopped to rest.

Brandon returned with the car, turning it around in the middle of the street and pulling up right in front before he got out. He opened the passenger door and moved out of the way. Zach used the car roof to lower himself into the front seat most of the way.

Brandon watched Zach get his right leg inside by lifting it with his jeans. The boy's dark brows drew together with worry. But he kept it to himself. "You in?" he asked Zach.

"Whew. Yeah."

Paula went around to the driver's side, calling good night to Edith, who still watched anxiously from inside the front doors.

"Call us when you get home," Brandon insisted.

She smiled at him. When he said that, he sounded a lot like his grandmother. "Will do. Thanks, Brandon."

Paula got in and drove off slowly.

She didn't see the two boys who watched Brandon from the shadows. They looked up at the sign over the Christmas House door as Brandon walked underneath it and inside.

"He got away."

"This time," the one with the blond mustache said in a low voice.

"I was about to jump him in the parking lot." The mohawk on the other boy had been shaved. His sweatshirt hood seemed stuck to his head. "Don't think he saw me."

"Guess not."

The boy in the sweatshirt scratched his scalp. "Do we need him to get in there?"

"Nah. But it would be fun to get him in trouble."

"You really think they're takin' in a lot of money?"

"I counted the people going in one time," the blond boy

said. "Five dollars, ten dollars—it adds up. Yeah. Bet it's mostly cash. Brandon oughta know where they keep it."

Paula was still driving too carefully for Zach as they neared her apartment.

"You don't have to baby me," he said.

"There are rough patches and icy spots."

"I don't think I would feel it if you drove over an alligator."

"Not a lot of those crawling around Denver," Paula replied in a light tone. "I think it's New York that has them. Anyway, hero, where do you want to go? Jake's place?"

There was a pause. "I can't stand his girlfriend. She thinks I wore out my welcome as it is."

"The heart-of-gold type, huh? How about a hotel?"

"A room will cost a fortune even if I could get one."

Answers she'd expected to hear. "Okay. That leaves my apartment."

"Yeah." He turned to look at her. "Don't worry. I don't have the strength to do anything that would upset you. And I'm not asking for the bed. I just need an upholstered surface to lie down on. A rug would even do. Throw a blanket over me."

"As if I would make you sleep on the floor," she said indignantly. "You can have the sofa."

They drove on in silence. Zach put his head back against the headrest. "Thanks," he said. "That'll work."

Getting him inside her apartment took a while. He reached the sofa and lowered himself onto it as Paula hung up her coat. She put away the basic groceries she'd stopped to buy at the convenience market en route. Coffee, milk, breakfast rolls. She had bacon and eggs. There was take-out barbecue in the fridge too.

"Good job," she said, returning to the living room. "Now let's get those boots off."

Zach leaned forward to untie them and gave up. "Oof. I can't."

"Take off your Santa belt."

He unbuckled the wide patent-leather belt around his middle, then slipped it off and handed it to her.

"If it's okay with you, I'll just leave the boots on," he said.

"Not a good idea." Paula pulled out a low stool and brought it over. She kneeled and picked apart the knot in one set of bootlaces and then the other. Very carefully, she eased the boot off one foot.

"I'm going to take a look under the flexible cast," she told him.

"Okay. Nothing hurts below the knees," he said.

She removed the other boot and used the stool to support his foot before she pulled back the self-fastening straps of the cast.

"Give it to me straight, Doc. Is my foot going to fall off?"

"There's some bruising around your ankle but it's not too swollen. You still have to stay off it as much as possible. I'm surprised they didn't give you crutches."

"They offered. I said no."

Paula just shook her head. Men liked to think they could walk away from crashes. A lot of them did—and then they keeled over. She skipped the lecture. He wouldn't listen anyway.

"You seem to know your stuff," he commented.

"I dated an EMT guy for a long time. Sometimes I went along on ambulance runs. I read the manuals."

Zach just looked at her. She could hear the question in his mind. *So what happened with that?*

"Neither of us was ever home much. So we decided to end it. That was a while ago."

Zach nodded. "That's how it goes. People move on."

"Other foot, please. I want you to be able to walk out of here in the morning," she said sweetly. She didn't want him to get too comfortable. Paula repeated the same exam.

"This one looks okay too. Want to keep the casts off for a while? Did they confiscate your socks?"

"Yeah. The orderly said something about a biohazard."

"Bare feet won't hurt you."

"I should keep them elevated," he replied.

He hitched himself around until he was in a better position. Then he stretched out and lifted his feet over the arm of the sofa, wiggling his toes.

For a few seconds, Zach just lay there in his red pants and jacket. Without the pillows to fill it out, the furry material rumpled into folds around him. The matching hat with the pompon had been left in the car. His thick, dark hair badly needed combing.

"Thanks for the help," he said, looking up at the ceiling. "Hope I'm not imposing on you too much."

"I'll let you know if you do. How are your other aches and pains?"

Zach sighed and settled in. "About the same."

Paula chuckled. "Poor Santa. Next time steer clear of the chimney."

"Very funny."

"Do you want to take a couple of those pills?" She had his prescription meds in her purse, along with his wallet.

"I guess I should. The ER nurse said not to tough it out. Hey, where's that duffel bag?"

"What duffel bag?"

"Mine. I must have left it in Jake's car," he grumbled. "It has all my clothes and a pair of sneakers."

"Text him."

"Not this late," Zach said. "I guess I'll just sleep in the Santa suit. It's roomy. I don't mind."

"Up to you. I'll get you a glass of water and the pills," she said, looking him over. "And a blanket and a pillow in case you need them. Then I'm going to bed."

"Okay. I really appreciate this, Paula."

"Happy to help."

She looked at the labels on the vials. He'd been given an anti-inflammatory and extra-strength painkillers. Zach would sleep.

She shook out the correct number of pills and put them on a plate with a glass of water. He propped himself up on one elbow to swallow them. Paula brought the bedding in and set it down by the sofa. "You're all set."

"Guess so. Thanks again."

She walked away, shutting her bedroom door with a tiny click.

Paula woke up before dawn, looking around at her room, which seemed to be much darker than usual. Drowsily, she tried to figure out what was different and realized that her bedroom door was closed, something she never did.

The reason why it was closed was snoring unromantically on the other side of the door. She got up and reached for her robe, tying the sash firmly around her waist.

Paula turned the doorknob slowly. Zach was sprawled on the sofa, still sound asleep. He hadn't used the blanket, just the pillow. The apartment was a little too warm. The colder the weather got, the more the heat kicked up.

He'd taken off the Santa jacket. He'd worn a black tank top underneath it. With one arm thrown back over his head, the rise and fall of his muscular chest was evident.

Paula pressed her lips together. He was out cold. She could treat herself to a good, long look at him and he'd never know. His massive body was completely relaxed and his breathing was steady.

The pallor in his face from exhaustion and shock was gone, replaced by a healthy flush of color. No more circles under his eyes either. His enviably thick masculine eyelashes showed up nicely.

He certainly looked comfortable. The Santa pants made good pajamas, with lots of room for those big legs. There was a gap between the waistband and his rumpled tank top that revealed more taut muscle and a narrow trace of dark hair that ran up to his chest.

And down. There was nothing naughty to see. But it was all nice.

Zach heaved a sudden sigh and stirred.

Paula stood still. He didn't wake up. He must still be dreaming. She would have to be quiet.

She moved softly over the floor on her way to the bathroom, giving him one last look over her shoulder before she closed the door and took a shower.

Paula took her time. She exited in a cloud of steam, wrapped up even more, with a towel over her robed shoulders and one in a turban covering her hair. One glance at Zach told her he was still sound asleep and not faking it.

By the time she was out of her bedroom, dressed in most of her uniform, except the shoes, he was sitting up, scruffing a hand through his tangled hair.

"Good morning. Did you sleep well?" she asked.

"Not too bad." He yawned and looked her over. "You going to work?"

Paula nodded. "But there's time for breakfast."

"Can I take you out?"

"Everything we need is in the fridge."

Zach shifted on the sofa, about to get up. "I feel like a mooch."

"Don't worry about it. I'll take a rain check on the breakfast."

"Okay. Make that a champagne brunch," he added. He rose slowly but he didn't seem to be in pain. "Hey. I can stand on my own two feet again."

"Great. But don't rush it."

Zach tested her advice by taking a few steps. "Not as swollen. The ankles still hurt a little."

"Come in the kitchen and sit down while I make breakfast."

He obeyed, taking the creaky chair. Paula got out eggs and butter and toast. "Scrambled eggs all right with you?"

"Whatever you're having. Don't go to any trouble."

She cooked; he looked around. The early morning sun brightened the kitchen with pale winter light.

The toast popped when the eggs were done. "I'm glad you're feeling better," she said, sliding the food onto two plates.

"Yeah. But I'm starving. This looks great." He devoured his eggs and started in on the toast while Paula ate her meal more slowly.

Zach waved his slice at her. "You're an angel, you know that?"

"Hardly."

"I had a great dream. A beautiful woman in white was walking through a mist. She came close enough to touch—and then I started to wake up."

"That was me. I took a long, hot shower and steamed up the place."

Zach chuckled. "Okay, so it wasn't a dream. But you did me good."

Paula got up to clear away the plates and start the coffeemaker.

"What now?" she asked.

"I'll text Jake, see if he can bring my duffel."

"Here?"

"No. The Christmas House. I want to drop off this suit. Norville is next," he said with satisfaction. "Edith said he'd be my replacement."

"He'll be swimming in it," Paula laughed. "But you promised her you wouldn't show up today."

"So long as I'm not working, she won't pitch a fit. I can call the insurance adjuster from there, meet him at the wrecking lot—if I can find a rent-a-car company that will pick me up."

"Taking care of business, in other words."

"Yes, ma'am."

He didn't try to wheedle another night on her sofa. Paula had sort of hoped he would. Having him around was . . . She searched for the words.

A pleasure.

Just looking at him sprawled out, big and bold, was a huge pleasure.

"Might as well get an early start, then," she said. Paula poured him a cup of coffee and set a quart of milk on the table. She went to look for her black shoes. She'd get coffee later and drink it in the patrol car.

"You bet." Zach added a lot of milk to his cup and downed the coffee in a few gulps, watching her run a brush through her hair and braid it quickly. Then he got up.

Bracing a hand against the wall, he inserted his bare foot gingerly into one of the heavy boots, then did the same with the other.

"How's that feel?" she asked him, putting on her shoes.

"Okay. But now they're too big."

"I don't have any socks that would fit you."

"I don't want to wear the casts," he said. "I don't think I need them if I tie the laces tighter. I'll just shuffle."

Paula stood up and got her uniform jacket out of the

closet. Zach squatted to deal with the boots, grunting as he rose again. He bent down to retrieve the flexi-casts and grabbed the red fur jacket from the floor, slinging it over one arm.

"Don't forget the belt," she said briskly. The sight of him standing there was a little too much for her. Even pulled down, the black tank top left nothing about his brawny upper body to the imagination. His stance—legs wide apart for balance, costume pants slung dangerously low on his narrow hips—didn't either.

Zach looked at the floor. "Oh yeah. Norville will definitely need that."

He found it and picked it up. Paula walked ahead of him to the apartment door, opening it and waiting for him to leave ahead of her so she could lock it.

He paused just inside the threshold. "Thanks again. You know I'd do the same for you."

"I hope you never have to. But thanks."

He still had the sleepy look and warm smell of a man in the morning. His blue eyes crinkled with a hesitant smile. Maybe he was expecting her to just shove him out the door.

She actually wanted him to come back. But not so much that she was going to issue an invitation.

Paula stood back. "Time to roll."

Zach pressed his lips to her cheek. He seemed to be himself again. In his half-dressed state, the brief kiss affected her more than it should have.

He went past her with the Santa jacket and belt slung over his bare arm. "Whatever you say, baby. Just ask." He chucked her under the chin as he stepped out into the hall. "I'm from the North Pole. I'm here to help."

Paula laughed as she pulled the door closed. Then she stood stock-still.

A neighbor in a flowered housecoat and pin curls was at

her open door with a female friend. Both women stared at them openmouthed.

"Good morning, ladies," Zach said politely.

The women said nothing. The neighbor gave Paula a hard look, then pulled her friend inside, slamming her door.

Zach shrugged his shoulders. "Now they have something to talk about." But he put the Santa jacket on and zipped it.

Paula glared at him. "I'm in uniform, Zach."

"So what? You're not on the job."

She locked the door with a jingle of keys. "Let's go."

"Can I get a real kiss?"

He just didn't quit. She put a hand between his fur-clad shoulder blades and moved him along like a perp. It took all her self-control to keep from laughing.

"Not now," she said.

Chapter 12

Out of uniform, Paula entered the Christmas House. It seemed relatively quiet. There were always fewer visitors in the time period around dinner. But the lull wouldn't last long.

Norville mumbled a hello from his customary post. For a change, he had nothing to do. He was deep in a paperback novel of Western adventure.

She ran a hand over her hair, which she'd unbraided and brushed. It crackled with static from the dry winter weather and indoor heat. One of these evenings, she would take a few hours to treat it with a moisturizing mousse and sit around with her head in a towel. She could even order up a romantic movie on pay-per-view, something she hadn't had a chance to do since signing on here.

Edith bustled toward her, humming. "You're early, honey."

"The sergeant is changing the shifts."

"Lucky for us." Edith glanced at Norville, who didn't look up from his book, and nodded discreetly toward the storage room. "Could I talk to you for a bit?"

"Of course." She walked with Edith toward the back of the front hall.

The folding table had been returned to storage after the

toy drive meeting but hadn't been flattened. Paula eased into a seat on the side, leaving the one that was easier to get into for Edith.

Edith sat and turned to close the door.

"What's up?" Paula asked.

"It's Brandon. I'm just a little worried about him. It's probably nothing."

"Seemed to me he was doing fine." Paula stopped, not wanting to give away that she'd met Brandon in downtown Denver to shop for Edith's Christmas present.

"Oh, he's keeping up with his schoolwork," Edith assured her. "And he has a new girlfriend. Nothing terribly serious. I think they're just pals. He met her here. She was babysitting two rambunctious little boys. Her name is Grace. Lovely girl."

Paula nodded. It seemed safest not to say too much. "So you've met her."

"Yes. She came over to do homework with him a couple of times. How could I not approve?"

"That's nice."

"After that incident with the other one—Tabby—it's a relief to see him with a girl who's genuinely sweet. And responsible."

Paula listened. Edith had too much to do at the House to ramble on.

"But that's not why I wanted to talk to you. He's been staying up till all hours for the last few days, talking on the phone."

"Yours?"

"You mean my good old-fashioned landline?" Edith shook her head. "He bought himself one of those prepaid cell phones with his own money. He gets part-time jobs after school now and then."

Paula remembered the folded twenties the boy had used to pay for the gift. His grandmother had inadvertently confirmed that he'd come by them honestly.

"Teenagers are addicted to their phones. Nothing much you can do about it."

"Oh, goodness, I'm the same way," Edith said resignedly. "I can't really nag him about it when I have both a cell phone and a landline."

Paula's reply was noncommittal. "Getting back to the late-night calls—did you overhear something that worried you?"

"No. I mean, I can't make out the words. He goes into his room after he says good night to me and closes the door. I suppose he thinks I'm asleep when he starts talking. It's always late at night."

"I don't know what to say, Edith. So long as he's not cutting classes or causing trouble, I don't think it's worth arguing about."

Edith sighed.

"What's on your mind? Come on. Just tell me," Paula coaxed.

"I think his father has been in contact with him."

Paula raised an eyebrow. She wasn't sure if Edith knew that Brandon had noticed the bit of news about his dad on Facebook.

"What makes you say that?" she asked.

"I tore a page from one of Brandon's notebooks to make a grocery list. And there was his dad's name, written plain as day. Lyle Clayborne. Several times."

"Why would he want to speak to his son after all this time?"

Edith pressed her lips together and swallowed hard. "I wish I knew. Lyle went his own way a long time ago. He wanted nothing to do with me."

Paula stayed quiet and let the older woman talk.

"Brandon is more my kid than my own son ever was."

"How so?"

"My ex got full custody when Lyle was ten. Just to save on child support. But by then Lyle was so wild I couldn't handle him. I couldn't afford an attorney to fight my ex, and to be quite honest, I didn't want Lyle."

She fell silent.

"That's a dreadful thing to say, but it's true. I was afraid of him. And I was so surprised when he came back as a young man. Not to apologize or make amends, of course."

Paula looked sympathetically at Edith. "To leave Brandon with you. How old was Brandon then?"

"Still in diapers. Lyle's wife didn't care."

"Now that's a part of the story I don't know," Paula said.

"Well, I'll just give you the short version." Edith gave herself a moment to collect her thoughts. "Her name is Iris. She didn't have family that I ever knew about. Came from nowhere, stuck to Lyle like a burr."

Paula asked the tough question. "Is she still alive?"

"That would be my guess," Edith replied. "I never heard anything to the contrary. Lyle has a half brother from my ex's first marriage, Brandon's uncle. He knows how to get in touch with me."

Paula let that go for now. "Was domestic violence ever an issue?"

"I'm not sure. Lyle had a temper. Maybe she thought of him as the strong one. I know Iris struggled with substance abuse. She honestly wasn't fit to be a mother, any more than Lyle knew what it meant to be a dad. The day came when they relinquished their parental rights."

"Does Brandon know that?"

"No," Edith admitted. "I could never bring myself to show him the official document or even hint at it. It would be such a blow."

"Someday you'll have to."

"The older he gets, the less it seems to matter," she said sadly.

"I don't follow you."

"Paula, at first I was afraid that they'd change their minds and take him away from me for some crazy reason. But they never tried. And now . . . my grandson is writing his father's name in his notebook. Over and over."

"Could be a passing thing." Paula's instincts told her it wasn't.

"I doubt he ever let go of the idea that he had a family—a dad and a mom—just like everyone else. I tried to be both to him."

She said the words with simple dignity. But Paula could see how much it took for the older woman not to break down and cry.

"He's a good boy, Paula."

"I know he is."

"I did my best," Edith said. "But when a kid turns into a teenager, it's like you don't know them anymore. They're on a seesaw. Up and down. Good and bad. They can't balance."

The sound of footsteps made her stop. Edith turned to the door and swung it open. "Who's there?"

Not Brandon, Paula prayed.

It was Norville. He held up printouts of accounting software. "Chuck Barbera may have gotten to the bottom of this, Paula."

"What are you talking about?" Edith asked.

"We came up short," the older man told her.

"By how much?" Paula suddenly dreaded the reply.

"Forty-six dollars and thirty-one cents."

She could breathe again. "Not a biggie," Paula said, relieved. "Two twenty-dollar bills and change is probably an error in arithmetic."

Not proof that someone had been stealing, not by a long shot.

"I would say that's very good, considering we're taking

in several thousand a week," Edith said with pardonable pride.

"I try to do things right," Norville said. "Now if you ladies have finished chattin', there's some kiddies out here who need that table to make paper-plate snowmen." He walked back to his post by the door.

Paula got up and Edith did too. The older woman peeked around the door. "There they are. Hello, children. We'll bring the table right out."

Paula tipped it over and Edith helped her snap the legs flat.

"Don't tell anyone what we were talking about," she said to Paula in a whisper. "I'm not sure myself. I just wanted to talk to you about it."

"I understand. And I would never mention it. Trust me."

"I do, Paula. And so does Brandon. You've helped us so much."

Paula slid the folded table toward the door of the storage room. "Count on that. And keep me posted on this, Edith."

"I will." She took the table from Paula. "Oh. I almost forgot to ask. How is Zach? I heard he came in this morning and left again."

"He's doing okay," Paula told her. "I know he had to meet with the insurance adjuster and go rent a car. He should be back soon."

She thought about him staying at her place again. He hadn't had a chance to ask. At least he wouldn't be wearing the red fur suit. But Paula had a feeling the neighbor in the flowered housecoat would remember him for the rest of her days.

"I understand that he persuaded Norville to play Santa," Edith said.

"That should be interesting."

"Oh, he's not such a curmudgeon as all that. Norville can be very sweet."

"If you say so."

He was now in charge of the Christmas House budget, and Paula had a favor to ask him. It would cost money. Not a fortune, but the expenditure was enough to make Norville start squeezing nickels.

Paula borrowed a laptop from one of the volunteers. The morning with Zach hadn't done wonders for her brain—she'd left her own in the apartment when she went back to change. She spent an hour looking up refurbished, relatively cheap machines that were suitable for an improvised security system. Her idea in the first place, and she'd dropped the ball on it. After what Edith had said, it was time to keep tabs on who came and went at the Christmas House.

She browsed and comparison-shopped, her face pensive in the faint blue glow of the screen. Paula settled on an electronics store in downtown Denver that had a good selection of different models and webcams and external hard drives to store video footage.

She sent the store's location and hours to her smartphone and shut down the laptop. It was getting late. Tomorrow would be a better time to go.

A heavy tread coming her way got her attention. Paula looked up. Zach was walking toward her, wearing sneakers but still not exactly light on his feet.

"Hello," he said.

He looked like himself again. He wore jeans, that denim jacket, and the fine winter Stetson pushed back on his dark head.

"Hey, Zach. How'd you make out?" Paula set the laptop aside. She stood up.

"I rented an SUV for now. Looks like I'm going to get a

new truck. The other driver's insurance company wanted to make a quick settlement. They made a good offer."

"That's great."

He set down the duffel bag he was carrying. "I guess so. I liked the old one. We'd been through a lot together."

She couldn't imagine being attached to anything with wheels. To Paula, a car was something that got you somewhere or got replaced.

"I'll get over it," he added.

Paula glanced down at the duffel. "Go ahead and ask," she said teasingly.

"Beg pardon?"

"Ask me if you can stay at my place," she clarified.

"Oh. That's not necessary. But thanks."

She felt a bit put out. He was turning her down when she hadn't even decided one way or another whether she wanted him to spend another night on her sofa.

"Did Jake's girlfriend reconsider?"

"Nope." He grinned at Paula. "She made sure I didn't forget anything."

"Oh." She slipped her hands into the back pockets of her jeans and rocked a little from toe to heel. "Well, where are you staying?"

"Here. Edith thought it would be a good idea. She just called me."

Paula looked Zach up and down. He did seem to have recovered his strength, except for the way he walked. He would do for a one-man security system, if that's what Edith had in mind.

"Does she still feel sorry for you?"

"I got that impression. Unlike a certain cop I know. So how was your day on the mean streets of Denver?"

"Tame. People seem to be behaving themselves this Christmas."

"Good to know."

"Want to walk upstairs with me? I assume you're staying in the attic room."

"Yes, I am."

She picked up the laptop. "This isn't mine. I have to return it. I was just trying to figure out a way to put in low-cost security around here."

Zach looked around. The usual line of restless kids snaked by the front table. Norville took cash and ran credit cards through an electronic gizmo as Chuck Barbera stamped hands. "Did something happen?"

"Not yet. But I want some kind of system in place. That way, we're prepared."

Paula went with him up to the room where the volunteer was working. She explained the security setup she had in mind as Zach listened intently.

"Should work," he said. "And you're right, we need something. Remember those two punks from the parking lot?"

"I do."

"I thought I saw them when I drove in tonight. On foot, a couple of blocks from here."

Paula stopped, holding the borrowed laptop to her chest. "Really? Were they heading toward the Christmas House or away from it?"

"Away."

"I guess that's good. If I wasn't off-duty, I'd go talk to them, ask them why they were in the neighborhood."

"You'd just get some smart answer. Brandon never did say what they were doing here that day."

She chose her words carefully. "He can be, uh, evasive sometimes."

Zach shook his head. "For what it's worth, he's been straight with me. I wasn't that friendly to him at first."

"You had your reasons."

They stopped near the end of the hall, looking into a

room filled with softly lit trees. The gentle melody of a Christmas carol floated out to them—until the wails of a small child broke the peaceful mood.

Paula and Zach moved closer to make sure everything was okay. There was a meltdown or two every day. Nothing new. Kids got tired and overwhelmed.

They saw a little girl of about three being held by her father. He stroked her hair to soothe her and she pushed his hand away.

"Put me down," she demanded.

"No. You're not allowed to take the ornaments off the trees. If you can't behave, we're going home."

Brandon came over. "Hey," he said. "Don't cry. I'll show you a magic trick."

She looked at him with wide eyes, but she swallowed her sobs. Her weary father hoisted her a little higher in his arms.

Brandon held out his top hat. "Watch." He turned it upside down and made a few passes over the brim. "Keep watching."

The little girl focused on the top hat and then on Brandon's smiling face.

Zach looked at Paula. "He does magic?" he whispered.

"News to me," she whispered back.

Brandon's hand flashed down and up. A striped scarf slowly rose out of the hat, twisting and turning in a lively dance. Then Brandon made the scarf disappear.

"Where did it go?" he asked the little girl.

"In there!" She pointed to the dark interior of the hat.

A few more passes of Brandon's hand and the scarf came back for a repeat performance.

The little girl giggled as she watched, until Brandon put the top hat down on the floor. The dad followed his lead and set his daughter down next to it. She looked into the hat and up at him. "It's gone!"

Brandon pulled the scarf out of his sleeve and waved it in the air. The little girl was delighted. Gleefully, she jumped over the red-and-white swirls and swoops he made with it near the floor.

"Thanks," her father said to Brandon. "Maybe she needed to work off some steam. It's close to her bedtime."

Brandon made the scarf disappear for the last time. He put the top hat on his head while she looked up at him with puzzled wonderment.

"Come on," the dad coaxed his little daughter. "Let's go look at the trees now."

She took his hand and went with him, looking a little wistfully back at Brandon. "Can I have a hat like that for Christmas?" she asked her dad.

Brandon tipped it gallantly to her as he exited the room, almost bumping into Zach and Paula. "Whoa. What are you two doing here?"

"Watching you," Paula said. She didn't add any explanation, and her answer seemed to rub him the wrong way.

"I know I'm supposed to be at the door," he said. The teenager's buoyant mood vanished in a flash. Brandon pushed past them.

"What was that all about?" Zach asked Paula.

"I really don't know."

Chapter 13

Children were scampering out of the theme rooms in a last burst of energy, shepherded by their parents. Several young couples stayed toward the back, each pair in their own private world as they moved slowly to the stairs. Paula had noticed that the Christmas House was more popular than ever as a place to bring a date.

You couldn't miss them, Paula thought. Starry eyes. That dreamy look. Arms encircling waists and shoulders as they walked. They seemed so sure that what they had would last forever. She wished the day would come when she could share that trusting closeness with someone . . . meaning Zach.

The House was a great place for dreamers. The nostalgic displays were a very attractive alternative to crowded bars and not-so-festive parties. She watched the last visitors drift past the door of the room she'd stayed in, the one with the softly lit trees and gentle music.

Back to the facts. She was reviewing a printout of their attendance numbers. More people came every week. They might have to go to a timed-ticket system to accommodate them all.

The weather was a factor. It had been seasonally cold, but a couple of severe storms would keep all but the most determined visitors away. Paula made a few notes in the margin of the printout. They could stick to the present system for a few days longer.

Edith poked her head around the door. "Are you alone, Paula?"

"Yes. Come on in. Just going over the numbers." She looked up. The older woman's face was drawn with worry. "What's the matter?"

"Brandon's gone."

Paula stood up. "I'll help you look for him. He has to be around here somewhere."

"I looked. He's not. Do you think he overheard us talking before?"

"No."

"Did you try calling him or texting?"

"Both. He's not answering." Edith shook her head. "There's something big on his mind if he up and left like that."

"He could just be sulking, Edith." Paula was inclined to take the matter less seriously.

"Where?"

"Maybe he went over to a friend's house."

"It's below freezing out. We don't know anyone in this neighborhood." Edith stopped for a second. "I don't, anyway. He might."

Paula nodded. "He could have called someone to pick him up."

"I suppose I should be grateful that my car is still in the lot," Edith said. "Did you speak to him tonight? It's been so busy, I barely had a chance."

"Just for a second," Paula said. "Zach and I found him up here when he was supposed to be watching the door. He acted like we were spying on him. I thought it was a little strange. I just assumed he went back down."

"He was there when people were still coming in. But not when they left. I asked Norville and Chuck."

"And I guess they didn't see him go."

"No."

Paula deliberated for several seconds. "Look, I'll find Zach. He and I can take separate cars and drive around the neighborhood. I don't think this requires calling the police."

Edith gave a sigh of relief. "Thank you. And, please, call me the second you see him. I'll stay right here."

"Of course."

Zach came out just as Paula scrubbed snow off a window to look into the back of Edith's car. She straightened when she heard his footsteps crunching over the light snow that had fallen on the asphalt. His big frame looked bigger in the down jacket he wore, haloed by the glare of the motion-sensor lights.

"Hey. I saw an emergency blanket in the backseat. Just checking to see if he was under it."

"Not there I take it." Zach frowned and peered in.

"No." Paula found her car keys and muffled the jingle by curling her gloved fingers around them.

"Blanket or no blanket, he could still freeze his ass off."

"Which is also true if he's on the streets or standing in a doorway. So let's go."

"Okay. Wish we didn't have to," Zach grumbled.

"I did things that were just as dumb. I'm sure you did too."

"Well, yeah." He headed for his rental SUV, tossing a few last words over his shoulder. "At least he won't recognize the new wheels and run away."

Paula considered the possibility that Brandon might do something like that if he saw her car. She quickly dismissed it. Yes, it could happen. But she didn't want to think about it.

"Square-mile search," she called to him. "You take the odd-numbered streets and I'll look along the evens to start. We can alternate on the avenues. Stay on the phone when I call you."

"I'll keep it in the cup holder." His reply reached her from the other side of the SUV.

She heard his door open and the engine start. Paula got into her car and followed him out of the parking lot.

A half hour of slow driving turned up no sign of Brandon.

"Hey. Pick up," she said into her phone.

"I can hear you okay." Zach's voice echoed. "Just talk. You want to go wider?"

"Not yet. I think we should go down the same streets, but switch. You could be right about him recognizing my car."

"All right."

Several minutes went by. She heard a muted whoop from the phone and picked it up. "I see him," Zach said. "Two buildings down. Standing in a doorway." He mentioned the street he was on.

"Is he alone?"

"Yeah." There was a pause. "I'm gonna double-park right in front. He won't see me get out my side."

Paula tensed as she pulled up at the end of the street. Zach didn't have him yet. It was unlikely that Brandon would try to outrun Zach, but he might. Zach still wasn't a hundred percent recovered from the accident.

She watched him go around the SUV and caught a glimpse of Brandon shifting his position, unsure. He wore the heavy parka he'd had on the day they'd met downtown, hood up, concealing most of his face.

Paula saw an oncoming car in her side mirror. As it slowly pulled alongside her, a leering face appeared at the window, licking the glass. She recoiled, even though she knew it was just kids being stupid. The face pressed harder and she saw a straggly blond mustache and lip piercing.

She recognized him with a start as one of the two older boys in the parking lot who'd been with Brandon. Zach had seen him and someone else on the streets tonight.

In the few seconds she had to take it all in, she noticed that the interior of the car was clouded with smoke. Faintly, she heard laughter from the inside. She knew the kids inside were hotboxing—sharing the high from a super-potent blunt. One cheap cigar, hollowed out and filled with pot dusted with something that wasn't sugar if the kids had enough money, was enough to get everyone bombed.

They stuck to streets that cops never or rarely patrolled. Just too damn bad she was off duty. One flash of roof rack lights and they would ditch the car and run for it.

She could call in the license plate if the car went around again. But the reality was that no one wanted to chase a bunch of stoned teenagers over ice and snow. It was next to impossible to catch them, and nothing much came of it, unless they were repeat offenders or had outstanding warrants.

Paula watched Brandon's gaze track the car. He stiffened as it drove past the SUV, then turned at the stop sign ahead. *Let it go,* she told herself, rolling down the passenger window to hear the conversation. If there was one. Brandon could just clam up.

"What are you doing here?" he asked Zach. The boy's voice cracked in the cold. But it carried on the still night air.

"Looking for you." There was a gruff undertone to Zach's reply that made it clear he meant business.

"You found me. Now go away."

"No. Not unless you can give me a good reason why you're hanging around here."

"I don't have to."

Standing on the sidewalk, blocking Brandon's way if he decided to dodge out, Zach peered up at the building. It looked like thousands of others in the older sections of Denver with a brick façade and overhanging cornice.

"Who lives here?"

"No one you know," Brandon said rudely.

Zach shrugged. "Just asking. I don't really care. Come on. Let's go back."

"The Christmas House is closed."

"Your grandmother's still there," Zach pointed out. "She's worried about you."

"She always is. Just tell her you saw me. I'm not running away or anything."

"Want me to tell her that too?" Zach's question hung in the sudden silence between them.

"Dude, I don't get in before ten or eleven these days."

"Why not?"

Brandon tried to make a joke. "Things to do, people to see."

Zach wasn't buying it. "You still need to get home."

"I will," Brandon said with exasperation. "Stop hassling me. Gram never does."

"Maybe she should. She really is worried. Apparently you're not in the habit of vanishing. Is this part of your new magic act?"

"Shut up." Brandon's voice was rough and raw. It was the first time Paula had ever heard him sound so ugly.

"You can do the talking." Zach stood his ground.

"I don't have to tell you why I'm here and you can't make me go back with you."

"Not by force," Zach acknowledged. "But maybe you can explain something to me. I saw those two punks from the parking lot earlier tonight. They wouldn't have anything to do with you being here, would they?"

Brandon was suddenly on alert, tipping his head back inside the parka's hood to see Zach better. "You saw them?" he blurted out.

"Yeah. Near the Christmas House."

Brandon tried to cover. "Okay. So what? I don't have anything to do with them."

"Do they live around here?"

"Why don't you ask Paula?" Brandon jeered. "All she has to do is look people up on her cop computer to find out everything about them."

"I don't think she knows their names."

Brandon's mouth turned down in a bored frown. "That's not my problem."

"Thought I'd ask, that's all."

Brandon looked past Zach now and then, keeping an eye on the streets as if he were watching for the hotboxed car to drive by again.

Drumming her fingers on the steering wheel, Paula watched what she could see of the standoff.

There was the sudden wail of a police siren in the distance. Uneasily, Brandon looked in the direction of the sound, then back at Zach.

"Let's go," Zach said quietly.

She wasn't that surprised when Brandon finally complied. Zach stuck close to the boy as he ventured out of the doorway to the SUV, grabbing the handle and scrambling inside fast, like he was afraid of someone seeing him.

Brandon pushed back the hood of the parka when he came inside the Christmas House. Paula had beat them there and gone in to wait for him and Zach. She glanced at Brandon, who wouldn't meet her eyes, and said nothing as Edith came forward.

The older woman was uncharacteristically subdued. She didn't fling her arms around him or launch into a lecture.

"There you are," she said in a low voice. "Don't take that parka off. We're going straight home. Wait a minute. I left my purse upstairs. Paula, didn't you say you wanted to borrow my camera again? Remind me when I come down just in case I forget."

Paula had almost forgotten. "Oh . . . yes. If you don't mind. I'll give it back tomorrow."

"Keep it for a few days," Edith said. "Unless someone else needs to borrow it. I hardly use it myself."

Brandon rolled his eyes, as if female conversation was just too annoying. He stayed in the entryway, leaning against the wall with his hands jammed in the parka's pockets.

Zach came in after him, whistling under his breath. He went past Paula.

"Good work," she said in a whisper.

He nodded and turned left to go down the hall, bent on some errand of his own.

Paula walked past the admissions table, setting a few things to rights. She could hear Norville somewhere close by, dealing with the nightly count before the money got bundled and bagged.

She heard a faint hiss and looked up. Brandon was beckoning her over.

"I know you were watching," he said softly.

"Brandon—"

"You made Zach go after me."

"That's not true." Not strictly true. Zach had agreed to search. Somewhat reluctantly.

"Just get off my case. You have no right to follow me around."

Stung, she didn't reply at once. Paula knew all too well how fast a nice kid could morph into a nasty one. It was happening to Brandon right now, for reasons she could guess at. She wasn't going to argue with him, not here. There were too many people around.

"You and my grandma are just the same," he said sullenly. "Leave me alone."

"I will. But cooperate. You have to go home."

"Like I have a choice. It's someplace to sleep, that's all. For as long as it lasts."

"What are you talking about?"

Edith clattered down the stairs. Paula turned that way, then back to Brandon. He'd flipped up the hood and moved away from her, pushing through the outer door.

Brat. If he ran for it, she would tackle him.

Paula stepped outside and went down a few steps.

Brandon pretended she wasn't there until his grandmother came out. "You and Zach can lock up after Norville's done. Here's the camera and the USB cord and the instruction manual. I put it all in a pouch."

"Thanks, Edith." She took it from the older woman's outstretched hand and waited on the snow-dusted stairs until the Claybornes were safely on the sidewalk. "Good night."

Paula went back inside. The embracing warmth took the chill away but not quickly enough. She went looking for Zach.

Chapter 14

Edith seemed like her old self by the next night. She didn't say anything more about Brandon then or during the days that followed, besides telling Paula that she'd checked with his school. He hadn't cut any classes or missed assignments.

He was less sullen than he'd been that night, but he wasn't all that communicative. And he wasn't at the Christmas House as much. For a few shifts, he didn't show at all and they put a volunteer at the door. Not in the top hat and overcoat, since his grandmother had rented both for him with her own money. Even if she hadn't, Paula would be inclined to think of the outfit as exclusively belonging to Brandon.

Paula didn't want to badger Edith about what had happened, and Zach stayed off the subject completely. They all had work to do that was more important than obsessing about a teenager's moods and bad behavior.

Nothing had happened. Yet.

However, there was an unspoken agreement among the three of them. If Brandon stayed out of trouble, that would have to be good enough. It would be great if he stayed out of lonely doorways, too, and cars full of creepy teenagers, but you couldn't ask for everything, Paula thought.

Norville's voice reached her. He wasn't calling her name; he was cursing a blue streak.

"Good thing we're not open yet," she said loudly. "Pipe down anyway."

"Sorry," came the grumpy reply. "But this getup don't fit."

"Let me see."

"In a minute. I ain't respectable."

Paula turned her attention back to the laptop on the table in front of her. A volunteer with a tech background had set up a wireless connection between it and all the re-furbs she'd bought inexpensively. Type the password and you were in. A few key clicks and every room in the house popped up on its own small screen, visible through built-in webcams.

She looked up as she heard Norville enter. "Can we rent a smaller size?"

Paula suppressed a smile out of concern for his dignity. "There's no time. But I see what you mean about it not fit-ting."

On Norville's lean and much shorter frame, the Santa suit seemed wholly different. The pillows bulged in giant lumps over the patent-leather belt, but his upper chest looked sunken in. The white fur cuffs hung down to the tips of his fingers.

As a final touch, he wasn't wearing the pants. His legs were covered by gray long johns.

"I look like an old Rhode Island Red headed for the stewpot. Skinny legs and all," he groused.

Paula laughed out loud. "You nailed it. Sorry. I shouldn't make fun of you."

"Just think about what them kids will say." He sighed. "What if they ask for Zach?"

"Tell them he's on vacation. But we don't usually get re-peat customers in the Santa line. It's getting too long."

Norville peered over her shoulder into the laptop. "What's that?"

"Our new security system. You can look into any room from any other room. Staff only, of course. This is the password." She found a scrap of paper and wrote it down for him.

"Hmm." He looked at the setup. "That's ingenious. You got video recording capability too?"

"Everything goes into a hard drive."

Norville looked down at the Santa suit he wore. "Is there a way to erase me from it?"

"Just wear the beard. No one will ever know it's you."

The older man managed a rusty chuckle. "Hope so. I'm gonna go put on the pants and boots. Then I'm ready."

"Okay."

Paula clicked out of the security screens and pulled up a photo app. She might as well download the photos she'd taken of Santa's first little visitors before she forgot.

She attached the USB cord to the camera and to the laptop, starting in on some paperwork while the app got going. When she looked up again, there were about fifty photos on her screen and more were popping up.

Paula knew she hadn't taken more than six or seven of the Santa line. Edith must not have downloaded her photos or deleted them from the camera's memory chip for a while. The shots all seemed to be of the Christmas House, mostly interiors.

She looked at the clock. There was time for a slideshow. No one needed her and the paperwork could wait. Paula clicked on a pull-down menu and chose View Full Screen.

It was a trip to see how far they'd come since the beginning of December, from empty rooms to sparkling wonderlands. Not all of the volunteers were faces she knew, but then she and Edith weren't always there at the same time.

The creation of the displays had been recorded step-by-step. Which would come in handy if the Christmas House was going to become an annual event, Paula thought absently.

Big smiles and lost tempers and a lot of hard work—it was all here. She savored every detail. Edith had photographed the more mundane scenes too. There was Norville at the front table, and then Chuck, and then the two men together, counting money like they were settling up on poker night.

Paula scrolled back to the first one of just Norville. Something nagged at her that she hadn't seen clearly the first time. She enlarged the image.

Her mouth opened in soundless surprise. In the background, waiting to get in, was the kid from the parking lot with the blotchy skin and the mohawk. Two visitors behind him was the one with the straggly blond mustache and the lip piercing.

In front of them stood Brandon, his back to the camera. He was holding up a hand. Both of the other boys, even though they didn't seem to be together, were looking at him.

Their tough expressions left no doubt that they weren't there for the displays. Paula's instincts told her that they'd showed up to harass Brandon or try to get in free.

She moved on, searching through the rest of the photos for more images of the boys. They appeared in several. Always in the background and sometimes with the hoods of their plain gray sweatshirts partially concealing their faces.

They didn't seem to give a hoot about the theme rooms or the visitors in them. The feeling that the boys were casing the house got stronger the more she studied the photos.

Basically, there was nothing of value to take, unless they wanted to steal just to get Brandon in trouble for some reason. Nothing had been reported missing or damaged, except for the motion-sensor lights that one time. There were no photos of the exterior.

Paula saved all the photos in a group, then selected the

images that showed the two boys, with and without Brandon, and saved them in a separate folder.

A gloved hand knocked softly on the outer door. Paula clicked out of the photo app and went to answer it. With her hand on the doorknob, she smiled at the bundled-up mom and the little girl beside her. More children and adults were coming up the stairs.

Paula opened the door. "Are you here for Santa?" she asked.

A chorus of yeses answered her.

She led the way back to the table and started taking admission fees and handing out tickets. A volunteer appeared to lead everyone upstairs.

"First group of fifteen, please follow me," he called.

Another volunteer appeared to welcome the visitors and get them lined up. Paula took the opportunity to peek into the Elf Room on the laptop.

Santa Claus sat lumpily on his throne and his assistants stood proudly to either side. Norville scratched his chin under the fake beard, not looking too happy.

The photographer crouched in front of him and took a few fast shots, making Norville blink until he waved the photographer away. The kids came in, looking at him with wide eyes.

From what Paula could see of Norville's face, he wasn't smiling.

"Hi there, youngsters," he said to one and all. "Nice to see you."

"Is he really Santa?" a little boy asked his mother. "He didn't say *ho-ho-ho*."

Norville scowled in a general sort of way. Then he remembered who he was and his expression softened.

"Ho-ho-ho." He cleared his throat. "Ho-ho-ho."

The kids giggled and he said it again. Third time was the charm. Norville smiled for real.

*   *   *

Edith came down the stairs, making a beeline for Paula. There was a lull in arriving visitors, but Paula knew it wouldn't last long. She didn't know whether to share her discovery of the boys in the photos.

Paula got a chance to think about it when Edith was stopped by a girl who was about middle-school age. She'd come in with her dad and just finished touring the house.

"Can I look at your charm bracelets?" the girl asked.

Edith had gone all out. Her wrists jingled and twinkled with tiny sparkly things on golden chains. "Of course."

"Look, there's a tiny Christmas tree! And a teeny wrapped present!" The girl oohed and aahed as her father waited patiently to the side, a smile on his face.

"How long did it take you to collect them all?" the girl asked.

"About five minutes," Edith confided. "Stella Bella Jewelry is having a big sale today. I stopped by on my way to the Christmas House."

"Dad, can we go there?" the girl asked.

"Are we done here?"

"Yes. I saw everything. I want to buy Mom a present."

Her father seemed amenable to that idea. "Okay. Good idea. I hadn't thought of anything to buy her yet."

"You're sure to find something just right." Edith helped them retrieve their coats and saw them to the door.

Paula chuckled. "That store ought to give you a commission."

Jingling, the older woman waved the idea away. "Stella Bellagio is an old pal from high school. We have the same taste."

Must be an interesting store, Paula thought. She had decided to go over the photos with Zach before she said anything to Edith about the boys. The older woman was in too good a mood to worry her. There would be time enough to bring up the issue, and it might mean nothing at all.

"So what are you giving Zach for Christmas?" Edith asked.

"I don't know. What do you give a man who lives in jeans and a Stetson?"

"A horse?"

"I think he has several. He lives on a ranch," Paula said.

"Oh, he did mention that once," Edith replied in an airy voice. "No plans to move to Denver?"

"Not that I know of."

Edith sighed. "You two make a beautiful couple."

"For now."

They really weren't a couple. That was a reality she tried not to think about. The passionate intensity of their physical connection didn't change the fact that the holidays would come to an end all too soon and then there was just January.

No one's favorite month, except for those hunting for a big discount on a washer-dryer combo.

"Hmm." The older woman smiled as if she knew something Paula didn't. "There's a dinner dance coming up."

"Oh?"

"Let me explain. I just got a call from the head of the Frontier Ball's financial committee. The checks and credit card donations to the Christmas House are all in and counted. Pledges fulfilled, every one."

Paula nodded.

"The final tally is something to celebrate, honey. The announcement will conclude the evening. I understand the chief of police said he wouldn't miss it."

Edith looked meaningfully at Paula's casual clothes and raised one of her neatly plucked eyebrows.

Paula sat back and folded her arms across her chest.

"When is it? Where is it? And why do I need to buy another dress?"

"You don't have to spend a fortune," Edith said in a slightly injured tone. She clasped her hands together. "So many sales. So little time."

"Okay," Paula sighed. "Just give me the invitation so I don't forget."

"Certainly." The older woman winked. "Zach already has his. I gave it to him myself. You can go together."

"Thanks for arranging that, Edith."

Edith gave her a beatific smile. "It's been so nice having him right here. That accident was a blessing for us."

"Zach is handy," Paula said dryly.

"He moved right in and got to work."

"Yeah."

"My kind of man. Back in the day," Edith added.

Paula pulled the brim of her cap lower on her forehead. The strong sunshine made her squint. Temperatures had plunged overnight and stayed there. She started walking down the street she'd been assigned to patrol, saying goodbye to her partner at the parked cruiser.

There had been a wave of shoplifting incidents and purse-snatching in an area of five square blocks. Mapped out and timed, the crimes revealed an underlying pattern.

They happened in the two hours between most of the schools letting out and sunset. The perps ran against the traffic on one-way streets to reduce the likelihood of being pursued by a cruiser.

Sometimes they struck more than once on the same street on the same day. The sidewalks in front of the more expensive stores seemed to be the prime hunting ground.

The victims were often elderly, and in a few cases, handicapped. Paula and the other officers had been shown surveillance video of a theft from a woman in a wheelchair. The perp had dumped the purse a block away and a Good

Samaritan had found it—and been incredibly kind afterward. He'd given the exact amount of the missing money to the woman, down to the last penny.

But the culprit was still at large.

For a few seconds of tape, the perp's face was visible. Whichever cop nabbed the SOB would make the news and receive an official commendation. Out of the public eye, the arresting officer would be taken out to Molly McKeever's pub, a police hangout, for free drinks and poured into a cab to go home and sleep it off, with the blessings of Sergeant Meltzer.

Paula glanced at the faces of the people she passed. Sometimes she got a nod and a smile from one or two. Most ignored her. Cops were everywhere at Christmastime, even in an upscale shopping area like this.

She saw a husky teenager in a hoodie on the dark side of the street and let her gaze rest on him a little longer. He wore wraparound sunglasses that he obviously didn't need to be wearing, and she could tell he was checking out certain shoppers and pedestrians behind the shades.

There was something familiar about him. He resembled one of the boys from the parking lot—if the mohawk was trimmed off. He sported a buzz cut that had been bleached in spots to resemble leopard spots. The weird hair had a purpose. The spots could be touched up with black marker in minutes, and he would look entirely different.

Paula looked harder and decided that it wasn't the same kid. This one had smooth skin, at least from this distance.

He started following a well-dressed woman who was looking at a smartphone screen as she walked. Paula crossed the street.

Leopard Boy saw her and dropped back, letting the woman walk ahead as he melted back into the crowd.

Paula had no reason to stop him. But she was sure he'd been about to grab the woman's expensive phone.

Paula shook her head. Smartphones were as valuable as

fine jewelry. There was a global market for top-of-the-line models. Cash only, no questions asked.

She was glad she didn't have to chase the kid, but she wondered where he'd gone. Weaving through the oncoming pedestrians, she lifted her head to see better. Her height gave her a certain advantage.

There was no sign of him.

Paula continued her patrol down a side street that would take her to a major avenue, also with expensive stores.

She spotted him again, from the back this time. A gust of wind had blown off the hoodie, which drooped between his shoulders. An angled shop window reflected his face, or what she could see of it, without the sunglasses. Paula realized a little too late that he was watching her follow him.

He ducked into a store. She quickened her pace without running and entered to find him gone.

"May I help you, officer?" a female clerk asked. She had appeared from the aisle between racks of women's shoes, one of several identical aisles organized by style and type.

"Did a kid just come in here? About so tall, gray hoodie, hair with spots?"

"I don't think so."

Paula turned at the soft sound of a door opening. The kid had dashed out from his hiding place and hit the street running like a triathlete, his arms pumping and legs lifted high.

Gone for good.

Until she spotted him again an hour later. The sky was darkening. Paula saw a woman fall to the sidewalk a block ahead of her, pushed by Leopard Boy. He stuffed her purse under the hoodie and tried to run, but a sidewalk vendor shoved a pushcart at him and knocked him down.

Concerned citizens caught him and dished out a little street justice before she reached the scene. Two men strained to hold him against the sidewalk.

Paula squatted down and worked fast.

"Let go after I get the zip-cuffs on," she instructed them.

A crowd gathered but kept a respectful distance. Paula radioed for backup. Leopard Boy lay on the sidewalk, his hood dragged up again but not covering his face. The sunglasses were on again, but the frames had cut his cheekbone. She looked at him as she talked. His chin was scraped. Blood from the abrasions was trickling through acne cover-up.

Paula put the two-way back in its holster and pulled out a thin rubber glove from a hidden pocket. She swiped a finger over the side of the boy's face, removing more of the beige stuff slathered thickly on his skin. Blotches appeared. He raised his head. With the glove—and no help from him—she removed the sunglasses.

His eyes were feral with rage. It was the same kid.

"I think I know you," she said. "You were hanging around the Christmas House a couple of weeks ago. What's your name?"

He snarled something that wasn't the answer.

"That's okay. I'll find out soon enough."

Chapter 15

"He's nineteen. First offense. Because of the assault charge, the judge won't just let him walk, but he won't spend a lot of time in jail either."

Paula was sprawled on the bed in her apartment with her cell phone to her ear, talking to Zach.

"And you're sure he's one of the kids from the parking lot."

"Once I saw him close up, without the sunglasses, I knew it. And that's not all." She paused.

"What?"

"I didn't get a chance to tell you this at the Christmas House. You were busy or I was and we kept missing each other."

"Just tell me." His voice was tinged with exasperation.

She wondered if he was in the attic room or elsewhere in the house. She imagined him raiding the kitchen. Then her mind switched to him in the old bed piled high with quilts. Big, buff, and ready to cuddle. Paula told herself to be serious. The adrenaline left over from the takedown and arrest was getting to her.

"Okay. I was downloading photos from Edith's camera—I wanted the ones I took of the kids the day you were Santa."

"And?"

"All of her photos were still on the memory chip. They downloaded, too, automatically. I viewed them in a slide show for a trip down memory lane and I saw both those kids."

"Doing what?" There was a sharp edge to Zach's question.

"I think it was the first week we were open. They were waiting in line to get in when Brandon was the doorman. They were looking at him. Not friendly. Threatening. He had his back to the camera, but it almost looked like he was trying to stop them."

"I want to see those photos. Can you e-mail them to me?"

"Uh, yeah. After we get off the phone." Paula felt around on the bed for her laptop. It was next to her. Sometimes she caught up on the news or looked at the latest in funny cats before she fell asleep.

"Were they anywhere else besides the door?"

"There were other photos of them in different rooms, generally in the background, taken around the same time. Edith had no idea who they were. Looked to me like they were casing the place."

"One less punk to worry about but even so . . ." Zach swore under his breath. "I think it's time the House had real security."

"I got the webcams and laptops in place."

"Yeah, I saw the setup." The comment was indifferent. "I'm talking about a real guard or guards. You can't do everything and be everywhere, Paula."

"No," she admitted. "I don't think anyone expected the Christmas House to make so much money."

"If that's the case, then the board can afford professional security."

"You're right." She sighed and sat up in a cross-legged position, resting a hand on a knee. "It's probably not a good idea to have someone as young as Brandon at the door either."

Zach didn't reply right away. "That's been taken care of."

"What are you talking about?"

"He texted me just now. That was actually the reason I called you."

Paula hadn't let Zach get a word in edgewise, eager to tell the story of the downtown bust.

"He said he couldn't be a doorman anymore," Zach continued. "Didn't give a reason, didn't say he was sorry."

"I guess that was inevitable," Paula said. "He hasn't been coming in as much. But I wonder if Edith knows he quit. She hasn't called and she would about something like that. She was so proud of him."

She blew out a breath, feeling angry with Brandon. It wouldn't help. She suspected he was still angry with her. And probably the rest of the world.

Paula swung her pajama-clad legs over the side of the bed.

"I need to give Edith a call."

"Okay. Call me back," Zach said.

"I will."

She paused a moment to think about what she would say before she spoke to Edith. No telling what was going on at the Clayborne household if Brandon had told his grandmother he had quit. If Paula added the news about the arrest of a punk Brandon obviously knew—and that Punk One had visited the Christmas House with Punk Two—the older woman would freak out. Edith was tough but not when it came to her grandson.

Paula went to the kitchen and fixed herself a cup of tea. The day had left her too rattled to think straight. She sat down in the armchair to sip the tea slowly. A half hour passed and she was no closer to finding the right words to ask Edith what was going on with Brandon.

She was overthinking it. Paula got up and speed-dialed Edith's number. It rang several times and went to voice mail. Edith's cheery voice asked her to leave a message.

"Hi. It's Paula. Just wondering how you were doing. Talk to you soon."

Paula shook her head and called Zach back.

By the third attempt to reach him, she was frustrated enough to leave a voice mail for him too. Maybe he'd gone to work out at the gym. But it was late for that. He could be at a bar, unwinding. None of her business who he might be with. He could be sound asleep and safe in bed like the good little boy he wasn't. But he definitely wasn't answering his phone.

"Edith didn't pick up. I'll try to stop by her place tomorrow." She hesitated. "Miss you. Big kiss. Sleep well."

She wandered back to bed, pulling the laptop to her to send him the file of Edith's photos. Paula resisted the temptation to scroll through her other, unopened e-mails. She shut the laptop down and put it on the nightstand.

"Phone tag is the worst game ever invented," Paula said to Zach. "Of course, it's not really tag if you never call me back."

"I was asleep in the attic," he protested.

Her new favorite fantasy. But she retained the right to be irritable. "And where was your phone?"

"Right here on the first floor."

Which was where they were. It was interesting to be the only ones in the Christmas House and here alone so early. Paula had awoken before dawn. Her phone was chiming with Zach's text as soon as she got out of the shower.

I know you get up early. Come on over.

* * *

The sun was bright but covered at times by scudding clouds in the morning sky. The wind made the sign outside creak and swing.

"I want to believe you." She was only half teasing.

"Get over it, Paula. I texted you as soon as I could. I was thinking of taking you out for that champagne brunch I promised you."

"On a Tuesday? Brunch is a Sunday thing. Besides, I have to work. I can't sit around sipping mimosas."

"You're right. What was I thinking?" That slow smile of his speeded up some.

It . . . was effective.

"So did you speak to Edith?"

"She didn't pick up, so I left a voice mail, asking her to call back."

"And did she?"

"Yes, but I was asleep when she finally did. I didn't pick up the phone in time. Here's the message she left." She took out her phone and put it on loudspeaker, then replayed the voice mail.

"Hi, honey. Thanks for calling and sorry I couldn't talk right then. I'm not doing too well but don't worry. Won't be in for a few days. Touch of flu. It's going around. Buy some hand sanitizer for the Christmas House and ask Norville to reimburse you."

Zach shook his head. "Tough time of year to get sick."

"I thought about calling her back, but it was so late. I didn't sleep too well."

"There's the bed upstairs."

Paula put her phone away, ignoring his reply.

"I'd have to show up at her apartment and risk getting sick to talk face-to-face," she said.

"Listen, she and Brandon must both have it. Best to stay away. I'm sure they're all right otherwise."

He didn't sound one hundred percent convinced of that. Paula had the same feeling he probably did: There was something going on with the Claybornes that they—Edith and Brandon—didn't want to talk about.

"I will," Paula said anyway. "But not for long."

"You're a good friend, Paula. Which is only one of the ten thousand things I like about you."

"Don't get started."

He slid his hand into her hair and lifted the auburn silk away from her face. She was in uniform, but she hadn't braided her hair yet. Then he caressed her cheek. "You okay? I get the feeling you think I wasn't here last night."

"Could we not talk?"

Zach took the request seriously. He leaned forward and kissed her lightly on the lips, then more sensually. It was tender and sweet and very different to kiss and be kissed in a room that was drenched in morning light. He pulled back and looked into her eyes, masculine pleasure dancing in the depths of his. Then he took her in his arms and kissed her again.

"Mmm."

"Like that?" Zach asked softly.

Paula nodded and turned slightly in his arms, enjoying the warm strength of his body against her.

"Want more?"

She shook her head.

"Why not?"

Paula nodded toward the front door. Her movement had allowed her a glimpse through the glass. Zach's thick eyebrows rose.

"Look who's here," he muttered.

Norville was peering through the glass. Evidently he hadn't seen them. They stepped apart and Zach went to let the older man in.

Norville looked sharply at Paula and then back at Zach. "I know why he's here at daybreak," he said, "but why are you?"

"Oh, I couldn't sleep. I have a key, you know. I let myself in and Zach was already downstairs. I guess I could ask you the same question, Norville. Why are you here?"

"The man is coming to fix that damn boiler again. Only time he had open today. Boilers are blowing all over Denver." The older man set down his thermos on the table. "Didn't you two notice how cold it is in here?"

"No." Paula looked at Zach.

"I didn't," he said.

She sauntered into the kitchen to make coffee before she went to work.

On patrol again, Paula and several partners spread out around downtown. This time of year, it was more important than ever to have cops walking where law-abiding citizens and bad guys could see them. The inside of a patrol car was comfortable but less effective for community policing.

The shopping area was crowded but no incidents reported thus far. One purse-snatcher off the streets didn't mean that much. There were always others. But today she hadn't spotted anyone who concerned her.

Paula took in the holiday windows. Edith was right about the sales starting early. She would be able to get a good deal on another party dress she didn't really need.

And there it was. Paula stopped in her tracks.

Her eyes widened as she looked at the cocktail-length dress on display. Made of shimmering white velvet with faint blue shadows where it draped, it was a stunner. The décolletage wasn't as daring as the wine-colored gown she'd worn to the Frontier Ball, but the dress was equally as sexy in an understated way.

Even the glassy-eyed mannequin seemed to enjoy wearing it.

There was no price tag posted. Paula noted the discreet sale sign at the mannequin's feet and the shoes that matched perfectly. One-stop shopping. She kept going. She would come back on her break.

What with one thing and another, though her patrol was routine with no drama to speak of, she wasn't able to return until the evening. First she had to quickly change out of her uniform at her apartment.

She texted Edith before leaving there.

Feeling better?

The answer was swift.

Thanks for checking in, honey. Taking another day off. How is the House?

It was hard to tell from a short text, but Edith hadn't answered the question. But Paula didn't see the point of badgering her about it.

Be there in an hour. Will let you know.

Edith sent a happy face.

About to buy a dress. What is theme for dinner dance?

Edith replied after a minute with a longer text. Not frills and furbelows. Very posh. White everything. Think snow and ice and winter elegance.

Paula smiled.

Got it. The dress I found is perfect.

A half hour later, she was in the dressing room trying it on. Paula looked in the mirror, turning for side and back views. "Wow," she said under her breath.

Getting dolled up was worth it. And getting out of pants was feeling better and better.

"Could you bring the shoes?" she called to the sales associate.

No answer. Paula opened the dressing room and peeked out, then stepped into the common area and padded through it in ankle socks.

She heard hangers on a metal rod being shoved hard and turned to see the sales associate duck her head and step through the gap in a wheeled rack, pushing gorgeous dresses to either side.

"Sorry," the woman said. "We're so busy today. My name is Marci. Did you need help?"

Paula smiled. "I love this and I'm taking it."

"It looks fantastic on you. And that's the last one. You got lucky."

"I guess so," she said happily. "I'll take the shoes to match if you have them in an eight and a half."

"Let me look." Marci stepped back through the gap.

Paula returned to the dressing room. The shoes quickly arrived, nestled in tissue paper in a designer box, pushed under the door by the busy sales associate.

"Thanks," Paula called. She slipped them on and admired herself once more. Her legs looked long and graceful in the nicely balanced high heels. She went back out into the common area and walked up and down. No teetering. She could even dance in these.

And everything was half off.

Paula reluctantly changed back into ordinary clothes.

She could hear the dressing rooms filling up as doors swung and hangers clattered. Women talked all around her.

She put the beautiful shoes back in the box and took them and the dress up to the register.

"Who helped you today?" the woman there asked. "And will this be cash or credit?"

"Marci. And I'll put this on my card." Paula handed it over without thinking twice.

The evening rush at the Christmas House was just beginning as she arrived. She hid the shopping bags in the front closet and threw herself into the routine of greeting visitors and doing whatever needed doing.

And now she could keep an eye on all the rooms from the front table with just a glance at her laptop screen. She did a quick check to see who was in tonight, noting the absence of Brandon.

Somehow she'd imagined the boy still might stop by, just to see the people he knew and pitch in, even if he didn't want to be the doorman anymore.

Apparently not.

Norville and Chuck were a solid team, covering their responsibilities without having to talk much. The box atop the table quickly filled with cash and had to be emptied several times into the hidden box attached beneath. Both men would have to stay late to count and bundle it into bags to stash in the safe.

The cheerful hubbub of children was almost deafening. Without Edith, managing the flow of visitors didn't go as smoothly, but they all got by.

Paula leaned over toward Norville. "Did the board hire a security guard?"

"He starts tomorrow. I think it's a good idea. But I'm going to miss Brandon and his top hat." Norville looked over his half-glasses at her. "Kind of a shy kid, but he did a good job. And he didn't seem like a quitter to me. What's going on?"

"I'm not sure," Paula said absently. The laptop screen and the milling crowd of visitors in front of her competed for attention. "Edith will be back in a few days. She'll probably fill us in."

Chapter 16

Paula treated herself to a day at the spa before the evening of the ball. There was no part of her body that hadn't been pampered. Her hair shone softly. She was definitely wearing it down tonight. Her manicured nails made her fingers look long and slender and sexy. Not suitable for work. But just right for a night out.

Still wrapped up in her old robe and fuzzy slippers, she kept the glamorous dress on its hanger and held it up against her for another look in the mirror. Paula sighed with happiness. Then she hung it back up on the outside of the closet door and set the new high heels beneath it.

Now for her makeup. The salon professional had showed her some great tricks—and sold her a lot of ridiculously expensive stuff.

What the hell. Why not end the year looking more beautiful than she ever had? She wanted to wow Zach, and it was worth the outlay in new cosmetics.

She arranged the tubes and bottles and tiny jars on her sink, going back out to check the dress tag to see if it was hand washable, spot clean, or dry clean only. If she got makeup on it, she could do a preemptive strike with a stain stick.

Paula knew she was obsessing. But the cocktail dress

was something she could wear again, maybe to a wedding. It would never end up in a charity bag like those awful bridesmaid's gowns.

She found the care tags in the seam. Hand washable and spot clean. Hooray. This one was a keeper for all time. The designer name on the sewn-in tag at the back wasn't familiar, but then Paula knew zip about fashion. There was a tag below it. The Iced Velvet Collection.

That described the material perfectly. Paula ran a hand over the shimmering folds, then went back to the bathroom, shucking the robe along the way.

She emerged naked. It occurred to her that she hadn't tried on the high heels barefoot. The last thing she wanted was an unexpected blister. She slipped her feet into them and walked up and down. Nothing rubbed and nothing pinched.

Paula caught a glimpse of herself in the mirror.

Her lustrous, carefully brushed hair fell over her bare shoulders and breasts. She ran her hands along her hips and struck a sexy pose. Without the delicate bra and panties she'd set out on the bed, she looked just fine. Fine enough to bring a strong man to his knees. Paula blew a sultry kiss at the mirror and kicked off the high heels.

Wouldn't Zach love to see her like that. Not yet.

She checked her phone. He'd sent a text.

Coming. Almost there.

Terse, but it made her tingle. Paula hummed a romantic song as she put on her underwear and donned the dress. The smooth lining glided over her skin as she tugged it down, adjusting the fit and checking herself again in the mirror.

She looked fabulous. There was no other word for it. She reached for the zipper and got it halfway up her back. Then the material caught.

Paula swore in a very unladylike way. She could rip the dress if she tried to wriggle out of it. And if she yanked too hard on the zipper, she could break it.

The doorbell rang. "It's me," Zach called.

She smiled wickedly. Help was here.

Paula went to the door, still barefoot, and opened it. Zach's mouth dropped open until she put a finger under his chin and shut it for him.

"Like the dress?" she asked sweetly.

"Yeah." His voice had a husky edge.

"My zipper stuck halfway."

"Really." He came inside.

Paula looked at his outfit. Classic black tie. Nothing flashy but totally elegant. The suit fit him perfectly. "You look great."

"Thanks. You too."

She turned her back to him. "See where it's jammed?"

"Uh-huh."

"Think you can pull it out?"

"I'll try."

Paula stared straight ahead. His fingertips brushed lightly against her spine as he went to work. The zipper jam was below the back of her bra.

Zach worked at it with gentle tugs. He grasped the little tab and slid it up and down.

Paula closed her eyes. It was fun to be such a tease. He wasn't teasing her. Zach was concentrating on the task. "There," he said.

She didn't turn around. The tiny noise of the freed zipper was audible in the quiet apartment. But he didn't zip it up all the way.

Zach slid his hands inside the dress around her waist. Paula moved her hair over one shoulder, revealing more skin. She reveled in his sharp indrawn breath, feeling the warm exhalation as he bent his head to kiss the nape of her neck.

"Don't leave a mark," she whispered.

"I won't," he whispered back. "You're flawless." He stroked her sides up to her bra and down to her bare waist, pressing more soft kisses on her shoulders and upper back.

She surrendered to the feeling but not to him. Paula stood tall. His caresses grew bolder, going farther down with each stroke, reaching the top band of her lacy panties.

Then his searching hands moved forward, sliding over the front of her until his fingers touched at her bare navel. Paula shivered with pleasure. He pressed in to pull her back toward him. Their bodies touched. Masculine strength kept her absolutely still. The sensation of restraint as he resumed kissing her was wildly sensual.

A low moan escaped Paula's lips. She leaned back against the powerful chest in the fine suit. Slowly, ever so slowly, he withdrew his hands. She turned to look over her shoulder. "Don't stop," she murmured.

Zach's eyes held a dark blue heat that could set her on fire. His mouth curved in a faint smile, then tightened. "We have a party to go to, beautiful," he said in a low voice.

"We have time," she pleaded.

He put his big hands on her shoulders and faced her forward. Then he pulled up the zipper all the way. "Maybe later."

Paula's disappointment must have shown on her face when she turned around. He stuck his hands in the pockets of his trousers, looking oh so gentlemanly. Except for the grin.

"I can tease too," he said. "That was quite a show."

She wanted to slap him. But she wasn't sure how to do it without leaving a mark. Since he had respected her request on that score, she would do the same for him.

"Glad you liked it." Paula tossed her hair back into place and went to get her high heels.

Chapter 17

A brand-new pickup truck was parked at the curb in front of her apartment building. Zach let go of her arm and gestured to it.

"There's my new baby. The insurance adjuster gave me the check yesterday and I drove it off the lot."

"That was fast. It's huge." Paula walked over and ran a hand over the gleaming finish. "Nice detailing."

"I can haul just about anything in it." He was proud of his new wheels; she could hear it in his voice.

"Including me." She laughed, her annoyance with him gone. "I love to sit up high."

"Go for it." Zach clicked the unlock button on the keyring remote. He maneuvered around her to open the door.

Paula stepped onto the chrome running board and hiked up her shimmering dress to get in, demurely swinging her long legs into the footwell.

A few passersby stared. Zach was a little more discreet about it. His appreciative gaze ran over her from head to toe before he closed the door.

In the several seconds it took him to walk around the truck and get in, Paula investigated the dashboard and radio and electronic gizmos.

"What do you think?" Zach swung up into the driver's seat.

"I love it. Has everything."

He touched a couple of buttons once the engine was running, and soft music filled the cab. "That's the idea. You can change the station if you want."

Paula shook her head and buckled herself in. Another great thing about the dress: the soft velvet didn't wrinkle. She set her clutch on the padded armrest and smoothed the seat belt over her middle, remembering the sensation of his hands holding her there.

It was going to be an interesting evening.

"Where to again? Same hotel?" Zach asked as he drove away.

"No." Paula got her invitation out of her clutch and studied it. "The Brevet."

"Okay. I know where that is."

It didn't take long to get there. The valet waiting at the hotel's main entrance stepped forward as the pickup rolled under the protective canopy.

Zach got out and handed him the keys, then went around to Paula's door to open it for her. She took his hand and stepped down gracefully.

"People are staring again," he murmured. "You look like a movie star."

They were. Paula avoided the curious looks, feeling a little awkward. It was one thing to play the temptress behind closed doors for Zach and quite another to attract so much attention in public.

Zach took her arm again, and she drew close to him as they walked through the lobby toward the ballroom.

A white glow emanated from the open doors. The décor dazzled her as they went inside. Waterfalls of light poured down the walls in an enchanting illusion of motion. Unusual ice sculptures shone in the changing light.

Every table was set with white pillar candles placed in real snow. There had to be ice underneath to keep it from melting, but Paula couldn't see it. Brocade tablecloths and napkins in a more creamy white gave warmth to the room. Fairy lights were everywhere.

"Your names?" The question startled her.

A man in evening wear had asked it. He seemed to be in charge of welcoming the arriving guests and directing them to their tables.

"Zachary Bennett and Paula Lewis."

She was fine with letting Zach do the talking. Paula was still drinking it all in. The catering staff had begun to serve champagne, and trays of hors d'oeuvres were making the rounds. No cherry tomatoes, no tiny tacos, no garlicky green pesto. Even the food was mostly white.

"Shall we?" With a nod, Zach indicated their assigned table and took her arm to escort her there.

They were among the first to enter the ballroom. All eyes were on her. There were looks of frank admiration from the men and assessing looks from the women. She could hear their thoughts. *Where did she get that gorgeous dress? How did she land that gorgeous guy?*

Paula held her head high. She set her clutch on the table. Zach pulled out her chair, and she managed the sitting-down-scooting-in business like a debutante.

She and Zach began to chat politely, as if the sensual embrace in her apartment had never happened. They drank champagne and nibbled on a few hors d'oeuvres, watching the ballroom fill up.

Paula recognized some well-known Denver faces: socialites, financiers, ski champions, and musicians. But no one she knew was here.

"Where is Edith?" Zach asked, looking around.

"I'm sure she's coming. You usually hear her before you see her."

The increasingly animated conversations in the ballroom were punctuated by the clink of glasses and lively hellos. The noise level rose to the point where they might not notice Edith's entrance.

A waiter explained the different entrées as new arrivals joined them at their table. Choices were made and introductions taken care of. The dinner was swiftly served. Paula made small talk and picked at her food, though it was excellent.

Finished with their meals, the other guests dining with them politely declined the waiter's offer of coffee and got up to walk to the dais, where a brocade-draped table was set up with microphones and pitchers of water.

"And now for the speeches." Zach didn't seem too thrilled. He put his cloth napkin on the table and leaned back in his chair, gazing at her and not the dais.

"I didn't know they were important people," Paula said.

"Me neither." Zach smiled. His intense blue gaze moved over her and stopped on her lips for a second. Then his eyes met hers.

"What?"

"You wouldn't want to get a breath of fresh air before we're trapped in here, would you?"

Paula shook her head. "No sneaking out. Let's do this right. There's going to be a big announcement at some point. I don't want to miss it."

"They could drone on for hours before that happens."

The master of ceremonies got everyone's attention, starting off with tame jokes that got scattered applause and moving on to introduce the VIPs on the dais. The conversations died down as people started to listen.

Then the speeches began. Paula saw Edith edging along the ballroom's paneled wall. The hush in the room prevented her from trying to get the older woman's attention.

"There's Edith," she murmured to Zach.

Zach glanced in the same direction she had. "No Brandon."

"Maybe he's coming later." Paula smiled at the other guests at their table. "Friends of ours," she explained.

Edith took a table not far from theirs, but she didn't see them. Her face seemed drawn and tired, but her golden gown made up for it.

One VIP after another came to the mike to talk about the Christmas House and encourage the guests to continue their support. Then the MC invited up a stocky man in a baggy suit and unfashionable tie. He unfolded a spreadsheet and cleared his throat.

"The bean counter," Zach whispered.

"Just listen." Paula wanted to hear what the numbers were.

"I am pleased to announce that the Christmas House not only covered its costs but also turned a profit within two weeks. And your combined donations will make it possible for the board to install new electrical wiring and renovate the interior. There may even be enough to purchase a new boiler."

Edith hooted with happiness and pumped her fist in the air, her multiple rings flashing in the white light.

Zach winked at Paula. "Good. Whoever is in the attic room after I go home won't turn into an icicle."

His joke stopped her cold. She hadn't thought about him returning to the ranch. But it was inevitable. She nodded without smiling.

The last speaker, a beautifully coiffed blonde, took over and got right to the point. "Thank you, Thom." The baggy suit retreated to his chair as she looked out over the audience.

"We would like to take this opportunity to thank all the volunteers and artists and good folks who helped make it happen, as well as those of you who gave so much. As you may have guessed, Denver's newest tradition is coming back next year. We are buying the mansion!"

Loud applause echoed around the ballroom as the speaker glanced down at the paper she'd brought to the microphone.

"Now. In round numbers . . . exactly how much money did we raise?" she asked when the ruckus died down.

There were whoops and even louder applause. "Tell us!" someone shouted.

"Seven hundred thousand dollars!" The blonde waved the piece of paper like a flag. "How's that for a fabulous Christmas present?"

The band launched into a swinging arrangement of "Jingle Bells" as many stood up and cheered. The MC wrapped it up and thanked the VIPs as the guests continued to celebrate. More trays of champagne flutes were served to all takers, small plates of dessert—white coconut cake and powdered sugar snowballs—were slid onto tables, and the party started rocking.

"Dance with me?" Zach looked like he was enjoying himself.

Paula was a lot quieter, her hands in her lap. She managed to smile at him. "Let's wait for something slower."

"Okay." He stuck a fork in the coconut cake and took a big bite.

"How is it?"

"Very good," he mumbled. "Try it."

She picked at a shred of coconut and left the rest.

Zach stopped eating. "What's on your mind?"

"Nothing, really." Paula stopped and took a breath before starting again. "I was just thinking that . . . it's almost over. The Christmas House, I mean. Taking apart the installations and packing up all the sparkly stuff is going to be depressing."

"Coming back next year. Bigger and better than ever, I'd bet. You heard the lady."

Paula looked toward the empty dais. The VIPs were mingling with the other guests. The number of dancers on the floor increased. She saw Edith chatting with the blonde.

Slowly, almost imperceptibly, the white waterfalls of light began to dim. Only the candles stayed lit as stars appeared in the ballroom's ceiling, which darkened to a deep, rich blue.

The band segued into slower music. Many guests returned to their tables, winded, but those who had sat out the jolly melody rose with their chosen partners.

Zach stood. "Come on."

She took his hand and let him lead her to the dance floor, threading through the tables.

The ambient light continued to dim as the stars twinkled more brightly than before. Zach took her in his arms.

"Soft stuff," he murmured as his hand rested at the waist of the glamorous dress. "What do you call that material?"

"Iced velvet."

"Really?" he said quietly. "It's so warm. But that's because you're in it."

The sensual rush of the embrace in her apartment echoed in her body but only faintly. She just wanted to be held.

They swayed to the soft melody, their steps careful, avoiding the other dancers. The band segued into a medley of different songs with the same slow rhythm. Zach and Paula didn't talk, lost in the music for a while.

Then he bent his head and murmured her name in her ear.

She came out of her reverie. "Yes?"

"What we did at your apartment—I think we should wait on going farther than that."

"Why?" she whispered. Until she knew they really had

a future together, she felt the same way but she hadn't expected him to.

"I don't think you're ready. I'm not sure I am."

Paula lifted her head to look up at him. His deep blue gaze was hard to read. If only she could trust him. "You could be right," she said softly. "Sorry I'm so moody all of a sudden. I don't know what came over me."

"Christmas blues?"

"Maybe."

They danced a little more and stopped when the music did, standing under the stars hand in hand. Zach gently pushed her flowing hair back over her shoulders. "Hey, what are you doing New Year's Eve?"

"That old song. Don't sing it."

"You know I can't sing. I just forgot to ask."

"Nothing." Paula didn't add anything more. She didn't want to do anything if the first night of the new year was going to be their last together. This time she led him back to the table.

The celebration began to wind down after another hour or so. Paula looked around for Edith, who hadn't come over once. It wasn't like her.

She sighed, catching Zach's concerned gaze.

"Do you want to leave?" he asked. There was no one left at their table to hear him or urge them to stay.

Paula nodded. "Might as well."

"Do you have to work tomorrow?"

"Let me check my phone. If there's a change in the shifts, we get texted." She took it out of her clutch and held it so he couldn't see the screen. Paula tapped it, not glancing up at him. "Yeah. They moved me to bacon and eggs."

"What?"

"Early shift. Very early."

If he sensed she was lying, he didn't seem inclined to call her on it.

"Okay. I was thinking we could go somewhere for a quiet drink but not if you have to get up at dawn."

"No. I probably had too much champagne anyway."

They rose and left the ballroom, occasionally stopping to chat with a few volunteers they knew. They didn't spot Edith.

But when they crossed the lobby and went out under the hotel's protective canopy, they saw her. Edith was huddled inside a bulky coat.

"There you are," Paula said. "We never got a chance to talk to you."

"Oh, I was in the lounge for a while, honey. Hi, Zach."

"Hey. Don't go away. Just have to deal with this." He turned to the parking valet and searched his inside breast pocket for the ticket.

"You okay?" Paula asked.

"I'm still not feeling that well," the older woman admitted. "That touch of flu turned out to be the real deal. But my doc said it was okay for me to be here if I didn't stay late."

"It was a wonderful party. And it's great news about the Christmas House."

Edith clutched the collar of her heavy coat more tightly. The rings on her fingers sparkled but not as much as her eyes. "Isn't it? I'm glad you two were there to hear it."

"It was quite a moment." Paula shivered and rubbed her upper arms.

"Don't you have an evening wrap or something?" Edith tsked at her.

"Nope. I wasn't thinking too clearly when we left," Paula said. Which was totally true. "I rushed out and there was Zach's new truck right at the curb. Have you seen it?"

"Here it comes now," Zach said, returning to where they were standing.

The young valet behind the wheel looked small in the pickup's huge cab, but he was grinning from ear to ear.

"Need a lift anywhere, Edith?"

For a fraction of a second, he and Paula exchanged a glance. She got it. They wouldn't ask about Brandon.

"No, no. I'm waiting for a friend. You two head out."

The valet had jumped out and run around to open the passenger side door. Zach handed the kid a five and came back.

He opened his arms. Edith chuckled behind the collar. "You animal. Go ahead."

He wrapped her up in a huge hug. "You're the best, Edie. Never change."

"You neither, kid."

Hug over, Edith turned to Paula for another one, not as mighty but even more heartfelt.

"Get some rest," Paula said. "Don't make me come over there."

"I will. Now you get her home and turn up the heat in the cab," the older woman said to Zach.

"You didn't say you liked it," he grumbled.

"Like it? I want one of my own. Drive safe."

Edith watched with amusement as Zach helped Paula into the truck's cab and waved good-bye as they rolled out.

Edith had to stand in the cold longer than she'd expected. Many of the departing guests stopped to chat with her, which made it easier not to think about how dizzy she felt. She gave them all the same line about waiting for a friend.

Her expression turned somber as she peered into the darkness. A taxi pulled under the canopy. The driver, who had a lit cigarette stuck in the corner of his mouth, peered through the windshield as Edith stepped forward and opened the back door for herself.

"Where to, lady?" He rolled down his window and

tossed the butt out, giving her a bored look in the rearview mirror.

"The hospital." She waved the lingering smoke away, coughing. It was an effort to think of the name of the nearest. She told him which one.

"You okay?"

"I'm going to see a friend."

"Visiting hours are over."

"Just take me there." Edith leaned back and closed her eyes.

Chapter 18

The emergency room was packed. Edith sat down on a chair provided near the intake line. She got up when her turn came to go to the window and gave the busy clerk basic information. She would have to wait again to talk to the triage nurse on duty.

Edith moved to a different chair. She held tightly to her purse and kept on the heavy coat as if it would protect her from the unavoidable noise and chaos of a big-city emergency room at night.

Perhaps it wasn't wise to have attended the party. But she wouldn't have missed it for anything. The emergency room was on the cool side. She shook a little inside the coat, feeling sick to her stomach.

A young woman in scrubs with a stethoscope and clipboard stopped near where Edith was sitting. Had to be the triage nurse.

"Clayborne. Edith Clayborne," the woman called.

"That's me," Edith said.

"I'm Jill Atkinson. Let's see . . . it's a little more private over there."

The nurse turned to lead the way to an alcove with two chairs, not seeing Edith rise unsteadily.

"Okay," she said as Edith sat slowly. "Tell me what's going on."

"I had the flu. It never really went away."

"Any shortness of breath? Fever? Headaches?"

"Yes to all three."

Jill Atkinson made notations on the clipboard. "And you came in alone."

"I didn't want to go home, not feeling like this. There's no one there."

The nurse paused. "I see."

"I really don't mean to be a bother, but I just felt so unwell. I was leaving a party and waiting outside and not even the cold air perked me up."

Jill nodded. "Sounds like you need to see a doctor. I'll put in an order for preliminary blood work, which the nurse will do. The intake clerk got your insurance information, so that's taken care of." She got up.

Edith grabbed the arm of the chair and hauled herself out of it. This time the nurse noticed her wobbling legs. "Can we get a wheelchair over here?" she called.

An orderly came inside of a minute. "Please take Mrs. Clayborne to Area Five," Jill said to him. "There should be a bed free in there somewhere."

The next hour passed in a daze. Edith's coat and fancy shoes were tucked under the hospital bed and a warm blanket brought for her. She spoke to the nurse who drew her blood but only briefly.

"Holidays are just nuts around here," the nurse said, undoing the rubber strap around Edith's arm after she capped the vial and removed the needle. "That's such a pretty dress. Special occasion, huh?"

"Yes," Edith mumbled.

"That's nice. Hope you don't have to wait too long. Doctor should be around soon." The nurse bustled out and jerked the curtain closed.

Edith closed her eyes. At least she was lying down.

She had no idea what time it was when she woke up and saw a white-jacketed young doctor standing by her bed.

"What happened?"

"You may have passed out, Mrs. Clayborne. The nurse who looked in on you tried to rouse you and couldn't."

"Oh." The bed she was in looked different. The rails had been put up to keep her from falling. She was also in a real room, not a curtained space in the ER. She peered at him over the top bar. The name tag on his jacket was blurry. "When was that?"

"About three hours ago."

She brought a hand to her chest and felt a hospital gown and wires. "Is that me beeping?" she asked.

"It seemed best to monitor you. The lab got the blood work back to us relatively quickly. Your body's fighting off some kind of secondary infection, probably viral in nature, since you told the nurse you were getting over the flu."

"Okay."

"It's your heart that concerns us right now. We'd like you to stay overnight for observation. Do you have a primary care physician we can contact?"

"No. He died." Edith smiled weakly. "I'm not trying to be funny. He really did. And I'm generally pretty healthy."

"That's good to know." The doctor turned to the nurse who'd just come in. "If you could provide us with more information, we can get you upstairs into the cardiac care ward."

Edith raised her head, frightened despite the doctor's calm tone of voice. "Did I have a heart attack?"

"No. Your heartbeat is irregular, though. That and the faint and a high white cell count are the reasons for my recommendation that you stay. But it is up to you."

Edith nodded. "I will."

The doctor asked her a few more questions, then left. The nurse behind him pushed a wheeled cart with a computer monitor on it beside the bed.

"We have most of your information, Mrs. Clayborne,

but we need names and phone numbers for your emergency contacts."

"There's my grandson. Same last name as me and he lives with me. First name is Brandon." She spelled it and gave the nurse the number for his cell.

"Thank you. I have that."

"He's only fifteen."

The nurse looked around the monitor. "Does he know you're here?"

"No. Actually, he hasn't been home for several days." Edith took a deep breath. "I'd better give you an adult to contact. Paula Lewis."

The computer keys clicked. "And how is she related to you?"

"She's a friend. And she knows Brandon."

The insistent buzzing of her cell phone was only partly muffled by Paula's bedroom carpet. It had vibrated itself right off the nightstand with repeated calls.

She patted the carpet and found it before the caller hung up. Not a number she recognized. The time on the screen was 7:46. She answered anyway.

"Hello?"

"Rise and shine," said a grumpy voice. "Pipe froze at the Christmas House. A patrolman spotted the ice around where it burst. The boiler is a goner."

Paula groaned. "Is Zach there?"

"I went up to the attic to see. Doesn't look like he spent the night."

"Okay. I'll get there as soon as I can."

She didn't want to think about where else he might have gone. Paula glanced toward the closet and saw the iced velvet dress neatly hung up. The evening that had started out with such high expectations had ended on a flat note. Zach had walked her to her door last night without coming in. Courteous. In control. Expecting nothing. She still wasn't sure how that had happened. She shouldn't have agreed to whatever it was he had said about her not being ready.

What she really wasn't ready for was to see him leave Denver so soon.

Paula scrambled out of bed, got dressed, and ran out. She didn't stop for coffee. By the time she was going up the stairs of the mansion, she had a pounding headache.

Norville opened the door for her. Paula went in, keeping on her hat and gloves. "Were you able to reach the boiler guy?"

"Got a different one. Maybe he knows what he's doing."

"We'll find out."

They heard the sound of a vehicle pulling up and went to the window together. A white van was at the curb. An older repairman got out and went around to the back to open the double doors.

Norville let him in. "Thanks for comin' out on short notice."

"No problem. Name's Al." He tramped into the front entryway and looked around.

"Basement stairs are behind that door. I'll go down with you."

The three of them went together, Paula last. The dim light made her head feel a little better.

Al set down his tool bag and took a look at the boiler. "What a monster. This thing's older than I am."

"We keep gettin' it fixed."

"Could be more than one thing wrong with it," the repairman said. "Burned out sensor, cracked gauge, who knows." He shivered.

"You don't have to tell us," Norville said. "We can feel the cold."

The repairman looked around. "You got a window open down here?"

Paula followed his gaze. A small, clouded window set high into the basement's concrete wall was edged with light, as if it was slightly ajar. She went over to check it out. The old thumb-type latch was dangling by a single screw.

"The wind didn't do this," she said.

The two men looked at her.

"Gotta fix that," the repairman said. "What happens with cold air blasting in is that the boiler starts to fire too high and too often. An old one like this will shut itself down. I think that's the problem this time."

Paula nodded. "Let me get a better look at the window from the outside before you do anything."

She went up the basement stairs and around the foundation. There were overlapping footprints in the thin crust of snow around the window. The exterior frame was cracked. It had been forced.

Someone must have known that Zach wasn't there.

Norville came upstairs when she called to him. "Was the door locked when you came in this morning?"

"I think so. But the key did take a couple of extra turns. Why?"

"The basement window was forced open."

"We were robbed?"

Paula didn't say yes or no. "Did it look like anything was missing when you came in? Any sign of a burglary?"

"I don't honestly know. Let's check the cashbox."

"You put the money in the safe after it was counted, right?"

"Yep. Me and Chuck did it together last night, same as always."

Paula lifted the tablecloth and looked underneath.

There was sawdust on the floor. Someone had hacked at the bottom side of the double box and cracked the drawer.

"They looked there first."

Norville bent down stiffly to see for himself. "Goddamn it. You're right. How'd they even know there was a bottom part?"

She took out her phone and called the station to report a burglary, then hung up. "Car on the way. Where's the safe?"

Norville rubbed his back. "Can't get into that with a saw. It's in the second closet and we padlock the door to it."

He led Paula to it and swore again when he saw the gouges on the closet door.

"Crowbar. Took the lock off clean. Don't touch it, please."

"Okay, Officer."

She pulled out a rubber glove and slipped it on to open the door, shoving aside a bunch of coats on hangers. The floor was bare.

"It's gone," Norville said with disbelief. "How'd they take it? That thing is too heavy to carry."

Paula stepped back. "Folding hand truck, maybe. You could get one through the basement window."

"There was close to six thousand dollars in that safe."

"They would have to be pros to get it open without knowing the combination."

"You think they weren't?"

"I don't know. Probably best if you don't walk around, Norville. Let me do a preliminary search."

He took a chair as Paula began to look more carefully. She pointed toward a little flashlight in a corner. "That yours?"

"No."

"Could have prints." Paula picked it up with the gloved hand and found a plastic bag to put it in.

"I didn't even see it," Norville complained.

"Could be nothing. Some kid could have dropped it." She had one in mind. A big, mean kid with a straggly mustache.

Two officers went over the mansion room by room. They came down the stairs, weighed down with gear and guns and making a racket in their heavy shoes.

"Lot to look at, Paula," one said. "There weren't any other forced windows, though. We'll file an initial report and get some detectives out here."

"Everybody sleeping late but me?"

Zach pushed open the front door. "Hey, Paula. Is that your cruiser out front?"

She jerked a thumb at the two cops. "Theirs."

"What the hell happened?"

"The safe got stolen." She put her hands in her pockets and walked away from him.

Zach followed her. "What?"

"Easy enough with no alarm system in place. The laptops were turned off. They're not set up for twenty-four-hour recording." She stood by the window and looked out. "And there was no one in the house last night," she said pointedly.

"Wait a minute . . ." Zach looked over at the policemen and lowered his voice. "I was here but not for long. I came back to change out of the suit into jeans. Me and Jake went out for beers. I ended up at his place."

"What happened to the girlfriend who didn't like you?"

"She's visiting her mother. Jake and I talked for a while and I fell asleep in front of the TV."

She blew out a breath and turned around. This was no place to air her suspicion that he hadn't been with Jake at all. "Whatever. Someone's been watching the house. They knew you were gone."

"Think it was those kids I saw on the street that night we looked for Brandon?"

"One's in jail," she reminded him. "But the other one with the mustache could still be around. Who knows what his name is. I hear his pal with the weird hair got lawyered up and shut up."

"Maybe we should ask Brandon."

Paula shrugged. "If we can find him."

"He texted me last night."

Paula just looked at him. "You didn't tell me that."

"The party was over. I was already at Jake's. All he said was hello, how are you, where are you, can we talk."

"Interesting," she said slowly. "And you said?"

"I didn't answer," Zach replied. "If you really want to know, I was bombed. We weren't just drinking beer."

"Too bad. It would be useful if we knew where he was last night."

"What are you getting at?" Zach stared at her. "He didn't steal that safe."

"I'm not saying he did. I'm thinking maybe he knows someone who did." Her cell phone rang, and she took it out of her pocket. "It's Edith." She answered. "Hello. Did you get home okay?"

Zach studied Paula's face as her expression turned to one of alarm. "You're in the hospital? You didn't get mugged, did you?"

He could hear Edith answer faintly. "No, nothing like that. I got to feeling sicker and sicker last night. It just seemed like the best thing to do."

"Did the person who picked you up drive you to the hospital?"

"Ah . . . yes."

"How long have you been there?"

"Overnight. The doctor wanted me to stay. Visiting hours just started," she added, a hopeful note in her voice that even Zach could hear.

"Is Brandon with you?"

Zach frowned as the older woman replied.

"No. He hasn't been home at all for a while. I'm so worried about him. Oh, here's the nurse. More tests."

Paula looked at Zach and shook her head as Edith murmured something not meant for her to hear. She came back on. "Paula?"

"Still here. Um, I don't think I can visit until late afternoon, Edith. Are you being discharged then? I can give you a ride home."

"Thanks, honey, but it looks like I'm going to be here for a few days until they figure out what's wrong with me."

Paula nibbled on a nail. "I'll talk to Sergeant Meltzer, see if I can swap a shift with someone else."

"My cell phone is right by my bed. Just call and come on up."

They exchanged good-byes and Paula put the phone back in her pocket. "I'm going to the hospital. I want to see her now."

Zach glanced over at the officers conferring with each other. "I guess I'll stay here with them. We can't have cops and detectives around when kids show up."

"That's hours away. I'll stop by the station after I leave the hospital." She took the bagged flashlight out of her pocket. "This is about the only thing that might give us a few clues so far. It's not Norville's and he doesn't remember anyone dropping it. So we dust it, lift prints, run them. Could give us our first lead."

"Sounds like a real cop show," Zach said.

"Excuse me? Are you taking this seriously or not?"

"Yeah," he said reluctantly. "I'm just sure Brandon didn't do it. So don't add him to the list of suspects."

"There is no list. When the detectives get through, you can board up that basement window."

"Those are my orders, huh?"

"It would be helpful," Paula said. "Don't hit your thumb."

"I never do. Not even with a hangover." He caught her by the arm. "You're not going to tell Edith about this."

"She'll hear soon enough."

"About the safe, yeah. Leave Brandon out of it."

"I will." Paula pulled free of his hold. "But I'm seriously pissed off at him. If he didn't do anything, then why the disappearing act?"

"Maybe he's scared."

"Of what?"

Zach had no answer for that. Paula brushed past him and left.

Paula picked up a bright bouquet at the hospital gift shop and added a vase to hold it to her purchase. She rode upstairs in an elevator to the cardiac care floor. The ward was state-of-the-art and relatively peaceful.

She looked for the room number the lobby staffer had given her when she'd signed in. Two more to go. Paula reached the right door and knocked softly, the gift shop bag in her other hand.

"Come in." Edith's voice sounded only half there. The bed was raised to a comfortable sitting position. She used the remote to switch off the TV.

"Taking a vacation, I see." Paula went to the sink and filled the vase with water. She put in the bouquet.

"Thank you. What beautiful flowers. And no, this isn't a vacation. I miss the Christmas House. What's going on?"

Paula sat in the armchair by the bed and told Edith

some amusing stories about Norville playing Santa. But they were both thinking of Brandon; she knew that.

After a while the nurse popped in to tell Edith that the doctor would be stopping by in fifteen minutes for another examination.

Edith rolled her eyes. "Help me escape," she said after the young woman checked her vitals and left.

"Nothing doing. You stay right here," Paula said firmly.

"Well, then, would you do me a huge favor and stop by the apartment to water the plants and make sure that everything's okay?" She reached into the nightstand for her purse and took out her keys, handing them to Paula.

"Of course. Glad to."

"I have to warn you that it's a mess. When I was sick, I just didn't have the energy to tidy up."

"Then I will," Paula said.

"I know it's no use telling you not to. So go ahead."

They hugged awkwardly. Paula straightened away from the bed. "Rest up. You'll be home soon."

"You bet." Edith settled back into the cushions and waved her out.

Paula returned down the corridor. She wouldn't mind having a look around Edith's place—and Brandon's room—while she cleaned up. You never knew.

Chapter 19

Paula opened the door of Edith's apartment as quietly as she could, on the off chance that Brandon was there. She called his name before she stepped over the threshold. There was no answer.

She entered and looked around. The central room was large and sunny, with two bedrooms down a narrow hall and a small kitchen that overlooked the street. The rental was part of an enormous old house that had been carved up into several apartments with odd layouts.

Paula set her tote bag down on a cluttered table and slung her jacket over the back of a chair. "Brandon?" she called again.

Her voice echoed.

There was still no answer. If for some reason he had come back, it was possible that he was here but asleep. The door to his bedroom was closed. She walked to it and listened. Not a sound from inside. She wasn't going to march in there. Yet.

Paula went to the sink and got to work on the piled-up dishes, seriously annoyed at Brandon's thoughtlessness. No, she didn't have the whole story, and he wasn't here to defend himself. But she might not have listened.

It was clear that if Edith didn't clean house, no one else

did. Paula had the dirty dishes washed and in the drainer in about five minutes.

She went at everything else with spray cleaner and a sponge, including the refrigerator door. Paula took a peek. The shelves were mostly empty. She would fill it with groceries before Edith came home. Paula surveyed the apartment, wondering where the vacuum was in all this mess. She worked off her anger by cleaning up the main room and making Edith's bedroom livable again. The vacuum cleaner had been stashed in a closet.

She dragged it out and got it going. In another hour, she was done. Except for the drooping houseplants. She watered them—there weren't many. Then she sat down and pulled her laptop out of the tote bag, setting the bagged flashlight to one side. She wanted to e-mail Larry, the fingerprint tech at the station, and let him know she was bringing it in.

He hadn't been there earlier in the day. Larry preferred to work late, staring into a monitor for hours to run checks. The man was a machine. He just about never answered his phone, but he'd do a fast check for her if he was still there. If the detectives had found other evidence, there wouldn't have been time to process it yet.

The flashlight could turn out to be completely irrelevant, but maybe not.

The sound of footsteps coming up the house's interior stairs made her jump. She tossed the stuff she'd removed on top of the Christmas cards at the bottom of her tote bag and opened her laptop.

The footsteps went in a different direction to some other apartment. Paula breathed a little easier. She wasn't going to stay much longer.

A list of wireless networks appeared on her screen, with a box that asked her to select one. CLYBRN2 had to be Edith and Brandon's, but there was a little lock icon next to it. Encrypted. No telling what the password was.

She picked up her cell phone and called the station, reaching an inside number. She knew hers would appear on the caller ID.

A female officer on desk duty answered. "Hey, Paula. Whatcha doing? Coming in tonight?"

"In a little while. Is Larry in?"

"Yeah. Working late. The sergeant wants cases cleared before Christmas."

Paula breathed a sigh of relief. "Can you transfer me to him?"

"You got it. Have a merry if I don't see you."

The transferred call rang. And rang.

Paula clicked on the file of photos from Edith's camera, on the outside chance that one of the punks had had the small flashlight on him. You never knew. But she didn't see it.

"Pick up, Larry," she muttered. "Pick up, pick up, pick up."

The phone continued to ring.

She studied the photo of Brandon at the door, his back to the camera, his hand outstretched. The mean looks the punks were giving him didn't prove anything either.

At first she had thought Brandon was trying to stop them. But he could just as well be inviting them in.

She moved to a photo of him that she hadn't paid much attention to before. Someone else had taken it. Not Edith, who was in the background, beaming at him.

Paula bit her lip. That kid was the apple of her eye.

With the top hat tipped back on his black curls and his wide hazel eyes, he looked like he'd stepped off a Victorian-era Christmas card, half boy and half angel. His youthfulness made him seem so innocent. Paula wanted him to be. For his grandmother's sake and his own.

Larry wasn't going to answer. Exasperated by the wait, Paula hung up. She shut down the laptop, sticking it back in her tote bag. She rose and put on her jacket, looking toward the closed door of the apartment and listening hard.

No one was coming. She went toward Brandon's room and knocked, calling his name again and hearing nothing. The door was hard to open, blocked by the clothes and school stuff thrown all over the floor. Paula looked in.

The bed was unmade, but no one was in it. The closet door was flung open; no one was hiding there either.

Nothing looked suspicious. She wasn't going to go through his things. Paula had crossed enough lines for today.

She went back to the table, picked up everything she'd brought, and left.

"HiDanhowareyou." Paula hurried past the night desk, not wanting to stop and ask the cop on duty if Larry was still in. The officer barely glanced at her. He was reading a newspaper, licking his thumb as he turned each page.

She kept hurrying through the maze of corridors to Larry's office. A blue glow emanated through the glass panel on the door. Paula knocked and opened it. He was there, in front of his monitor.

"Larry, glad I caught you." She moved swiftly to his desk.

"Hi, Paula."

She set her tote bag on his desk and took out the bagged flashlight.

"I need you to dust this and run the prints."

"Okay."

The flat reply meant he would help. Larry just wasn't the demonstrative type. You never had to waste time on small talk, because he told chatterboxes point-blank to shut up so he could concentrate. He was amazingly good at his job.

He got up and pulled on rubber gloves, unpacking a kit and setting it on a counter.

Paula watched his meticulous work as he dusted the flashlight and examined it under a magnifying lamp for prints.

"Got some," he said. She nodded.

He used tape to lift two that were close together and then the third. There was a faint smile on his face. "Nice and sharp. Look at those whorls."

Larry lived for whorls.

"Handled with care at the scene," Paula said.

That was way too many words for Larry, who shot her a look. Then he went back to processing the prints. He scanned them and ran them.

Paula knew the national database was fast, but tonight it seemed slow. Larry didn't say anything as they waited.

Several possible matches appeared. Larry enlarged each one by one, studying the screen. The clicking mouse made the only sound in the room.

He pointed. "That one."

Paula looked over his shoulder. They all looked identical to her, but she wasn't the expert.

"You want the whole shebang?"

As in name, aliases, mug shot, tattoos, piercings, criminal record linked to the fingerprints on file, driver's license, and car registration, if any. "Yes," she said excitedly.

He pulled up the information. Paula looked at the face in the mug shot.

Straggly blond mustache. An ugly stud through the upper lip. Straw-colored dirty hair that she'd never seen because the kid's hood had always been up.

But he wasn't a juvenile. He was nineteen. And he had a record as an adult.

"That your man?"

Paula kept her voice level. "Yes."

"Want a printout?"

"If you would."

Larry sent all the information to the printer and pulled out each page in the same methodical way he'd handled the fingerprint processing. He stacked and stapled the sheets and handed them to her.

"Fantastic." She flipped through the pages, quickly absorbing a lot of the information. Exactly what she'd hoped for. Paula looked up. Larry had already returned to his monitor and was sitting in front of it, absorbed in something else.

"Thanks again," she called to him as she exited. He didn't turn his head.

She went back to the cubicle area, looking for one that hadn't been assigned to anyone. She wanted to get on this.

"Here comes Little Miss Cop." Paula knew who was talking. Detective Robson of the carefully styled pompadour and expensive ties. "Heard you were at the Christmas House this morning. I got there after you left."

Had to be long after she'd left, Paula thought, as she went by him. "Really." The only available empty cubicle was next to his. She took it.

"Eager beaver."

"You know what they say about the first forty-eight hours. The trail gets cold fast after that. People leave town. Evidence disappears."

Robson was leaning back in his swivel chair. "We didn't find anything, so we adjourned to Hanrahan's to discuss the case."

Over steaks and single malt. He was famous for letting the evidence techs do all the work at a crime scene and taking the credit himself.

"Might have another look-see tomorrow, though. What was in that safe, six, seven grand? Only money, right? No one got hurt."

"Let's hope not."

He clasped his hands behind his head and leaned back. "Wow. You sound like you want to get involved."

"It's personal, Robson. I want to work on it." She turned away from him and opened her laptop, logging on with the station password.

His phone rang. The detective waited before picking it up. "Robson. Where? Shoot. That's all the way across town. All right. See you."

Paula silently thanked the perps, whoever they were.

Zach called her at her apartment the next morning. "How's Edith doing?"

Considering that she and Zach had had a difference of opinion over Brandon, Paula was glad he'd chosen that for an opener.

"She seemed all right. She called me last night, said she was bored to pieces but they're not letting her go just yet."

"That's good news in a way." He paused. "Did Brandon ever show?"

"No. And he won't return her calls. However, she won't tell him she's in the hospital. She doesn't want him to worry."

Zach sighed. "Maybe I should text him."

Paula seized the chance. "I was going to ask you to."

"Whoa. What for?"

"I just need to talk to him."

"Dammit, Paula, I don't think he had anything to do with the theft of the safe. I trust him, even if you don't. Have a little faith in the kid."

Paula ignored the dig. "Let me bring you up to date. The fingerprints on the flashlight belonged to one person. Not him."

"Well. So he's cleared."

Not yet. Paula didn't want to start another argument with Zach, not when she needed his help. She didn't reply.

"Who was it?" Zach asked.

"That blond kid. His name is Otis Parker. He has a record."

"As a juvenile?"

Paula smiled to herself. "You're picking up the lingo.

No. As an adult. He's nineteen. But we can't get a warrant for him for just the fingerprints. We're looking for his car, checking out his addresses in Denver, the usual."

"Okay."

"So . . . if Brandon could give us more information, it might speed things up."

Zach thought it over. "Call him yourself, Paula. I'm not comfortable with doing it for you."

They were back where they'd started. "I guess you don't trust me."

"About as much as you trust me. I know you don't believe I was with Jake the other night."

"You're right. Good-bye." Paula hung up on him. She was steamed.

If she never saw him again, that would work for her. So much for that whirlwind romance.

Edith had given her yet another prepaid number for Brandon. She sent a text and left him a longer voice mail for good measure.

"Brandon, it's Paula. I don't know where you are, but I have to talk to you. Your grandmother's in the hospital—under observation. She may be there for a few days. Get back to me."

She set down the phone and went to make herself a cup of tea.

It rang an hour later.

"Paula. It's me. What's going on? What's the matter with Gram?"

"Something with her heart. They're running tests and no, she didn't have a heart attack. She doesn't want you to worry. I think it's time you did."

Brandon was silent for a little too long.

"Don't you dare hang up on me," Paula said tightly. "I want to talk to you."

"Where?"

The first crack in the wall had opened. Good.

"The Christmas House."

She heard someone talking in the background. Brandon must have put a hand over the phone. The words were muffled, but the voice was female and young.

"Okay. I don't have another place we could go."

That reminded Paula of another question that needed asking.

"Mind telling me where you've been shacking up, Brandon?"

To her surprise, he gave her a straight answer. "At a youth shelter."

"And who were you just talking to?"

"Grace. She keeps telling me to go home."

Paula nodded. "I like that girl. And that's good advice. Can you be at the Christmas House tomorrow morning by eight?"

"Okay. They kick us out by seven anyway."

Paula didn't bother to notify Zach that she was meeting Brandon. She was still angry with him.

The smell of coffee was coming from the kitchen when she let herself in. The Christmas House looked about the same, outside and in. She'd noticed coming up the stairs that the ice from the flood of the busted pipe had been chipped away. She wondered if Zach had seen to the basement window. She would go down and take a look to make sure.

She hung up her coat. Zach came out of the kitchen with a mug of coffee.

"Good morning." His voice was casual, as if she hadn't hung up on him the night before.

"Hello."

He took a sip and set the mug down on the front table. "Anything you want to tell me?"

"No new developments, if that's what you mean," she said. "No one's been charged."

Zach folded his arms over his chest and looked at her. His gaze was as calm as his voice. It unsettled her. Paula tried to think of a way to get him to leave.

"I know why you're here," he said at last. "Brandon told me."

She hadn't thought of that. "Oh. Then obviously you know I called him. He agreed to meet me. He should be here soon." There was no need to say any more than that.

"You talking to him as a friend or as a cop?"

His gaze had narrowed on her. Paula found it hard to believe that she'd thought of him as easygoing. Not at the moment, that was for damn sure.

"I'm off duty. And he's not a suspect."

Zach nodded. He turned his head at the sound of the outside door opening. Paula had left it unlocked. Brandon came in. He looked at Zach first, then at Paula.

"Okay," he said to her. "Here I am."

Chapter 20

Brandon didn't look like an angel this morning. His black curls were matted and his eyes had dark circles under them. Staying at a shelter was rough. Her heart went out to him.

"Good to see you, Brandon." Zach made no comment on the boy's appearance as he glanced at his wrinkled clothes. He picked up his cup. "Talk to me before you go, okay?"

Brandon nodded, running a hand through his hair. Even his fingernails were dirty, Paula noticed.

Zach finished his coffee and went toward the kitchen. He came out without the cup, changed direction, and headed toward the door that led to the basement stairs. "Almost forgot," he said to Paula. "I have to fix the window."

"You do that," she replied. She didn't know if he'd told Brandon about the robbery and the missing safe. He had no right to.

Zach turned again and headed for the central staircase. "Oops. Left my tools in the Elf Room."

Paula had a feeling he was up to something.

"We can talk in the reception room, Brandon," she said. "There are comfortable chairs in there."

"All right. Then I want to go see Gram. She was so happy when I called just now. I felt really bad."

Paula refrained from telling him that he damn well should.

"Do you want some coffee?"

"No. I'm kinda sick to my stomach. The shelter hands out hot dishwater and stale pastry. I had both."

She hoped he'd learned a lesson or two. So many of the homeless kids on the streets wanted to go home again and couldn't. Paula kept that to herself too.

They went in and got settled. He slumped way down in the chair, resting his head against the amply stuffed back with a sigh. "Wow. This is comfortable."

Paula looked at him.

"Am I going to get a lecture?" he said, gazing at the ceiling. "I don't care. It's warm in here."

"No. Like I said, I just wanted to talk to you. And I'm really glad you're going to see your grandmother, by the way. I know things have been difficult, but there's not much I can do about that."

"I just want everyone to leave me alone."

"Yes, well, you do have a family, and other people who worry about you, too, Brandon."

"Guess so. But Gram is the only one who cares about me."

Paula just wished she knew a way to get him to reciprocate. But at least he had answered her call. That was a step forward. A small one.

"Let's talk about that later."

"Okay," he mumbled, sinking deeper into the chair.

"I don't know if Zach told you, but the Christmas House was robbed night before last."

Brandon looked at her with wide eyes. "No. He didn't say anything. Who would do that? What got stolen?"

"The safe. It had a lot of money in it. But someone sawed open the cashbox first."

Brandon's tired mouth turned down in an angry scowl as he cursed. "I helped Zach build that."

"I know."

Paula took a deep breath.

"Don't look at me like that." Brandon shook his head. "I didn't do it."

"We have a solid lead on the person who did. I think you know him."

She took the mug shot from her tote bag.

"Otis. I don't know his last name." Brandon stared at the photo with disgust. "But yeah. He and that other guy were asking me about the House. Then they tried to get in for free."

"They managed it somehow. Both of them appeared in photos on your grandmother's camera. Not that she was trying to take pictures of them. They were just in the background."

Brandon shrugged. "They paid. I couldn't stop them. That was a while ago."

"I know." Paula wasn't done. She remembered him huddled in the doorway the night she and Zach had found him. "There's something else. Did you . . . Were they harassing you or bullying you?"

"Sort of. Sometimes. That's what they do. I'm not the only one they pick on. Basically, I dodged them." He shot a sideways look at her. "That night you and Zach came upstairs? I was trying to stay away from them."

She and Zach had put him in harm's way by making him go back to the door. As if the kid wasn't mixed up enough already. She felt a pang of regret.

"Why didn't you tell us what was going on?"

"You guys have enough to do. I felt like they came around because I was there."

"There's probably some truth in that," Paula said. "But you weren't to blame."

"Yeah. Maybe not. I went out once I saw they were gone. I was just standing there and they drove by, acting like idiots." He paused, remembering. "I do have a friend in that building where you found me. He wasn't home."

His exhaustion was plain. Paula felt bad asking him questions.

"Otis and those other kids followed me. You and Zach followed me. It was just weird. That's why I was snotty to you about it."

It wasn't an apology, but at least it was an explanation.

"I didn't take it too seriously," she said.

Brandon gave her a sullen look. "You probably think I deal drugs or something."

Paula shook her head. "No. I mean, they were high but you didn't seem to be."

Brandon studied her as if he were about to share something. He hesitated, then said, "There has to be a reason you thought I could do something like boost a safe."

"I never thought you stole the safe." Paula chose her next words carefully. "But there was something else. Before the safe got stolen, Norville came up short when the money was counted. It turned out to be no big deal—the difference was forty bucks and change."

"But I built the box. So, like, you thought I did that to steal?" Brandon sat up. "Some friend you are."

She was on the spot. "I'll be honest. I did think that for about five seconds. We went shopping for your grandma's Christmas present and you had all that cash. I'm a cop. I can't help it. Come on, Brandon. Cut me some slack here. You have been in trouble."

He just stared at her, a dull look in his eyes.

"Yeah. Not for anything like that."

"I'm sorry I mentioned it."

Brandon hung his head. "Like hell. But bring it on. That can't be all."

"You texted Zach the night the safe was stolen. Whoever did it knew he wasn't there. Where were you?"

"At home. I came in after Gram went out to that dumb party. I left before the time I figured she'd come back."

The time frame didn't quite fit. He'd tried to reach Zach late at night, later than that. "Was there anyone with you?"

"No."

He didn't have an alibi. But Paula felt he was telling the truth. Every cop knew that the truth never was carved in stone and details were never perfectly consistent.

Brandon got up. "No matter what I say, you don't really believe me. Screw this. Screw you."

"Don't talk to me like that."

"Screw everything." He reached the door before she could scramble to her feet. "I'm going to see Gram."

Chapter 21

Zach came down the stairs in time to see Brandon slam out the door.

"Don't go after him," Paula said.

He stopped by the front table and turned to her with a look of pure exasperation. "What the hell did you think you were doing? That comment about where he got the money was totally out of line."

Paula was taken aback. "You were listening?"

"Touch one key. Every room is visible from every other room."

Her laptop security system. He hadn't sounded too impressed with it a week ago. Evidently he knew how to use it now and had obviously added a downloaded app to record sound. "Thanks for snooping."

"It doesn't matter, Paula."

"Oh yes, it does," she snapped.

He walked toward her, fiery blue anger in his eyes. Paula stood her ground.

"I can tell you where he got the money for Edith's present. Brandon asked me about part-time work after school and I sent him to Jake. That kid hauled lumber and pulled nails at a construction site for two days. He worked like a dog. Jake paid him off the books in cash."

"So why didn't he tell me?"

"Because he's underage and couldn't get a work permit for a job like that," Zach answered in a growl. "So he broke the goddamn law and so did Jake and I guess you could say I was an accessory."

"He could have asked me if he needed money. I was ready to help him pay for his grandma's present."

"The kid has pride. He wanted to buy you a present too. I helped him shop for it. He swore me to secrecy."

Paula stepped back. "Oh."

"He thinks you walk on water."

"Could have fooled me," she said.

"Don't know how you missed it. I felt the same way watching you in action. Never knew a woman who could get so much done and look so damn good doing it. However, he thought of you like a big sister."

She barely heard what he was saying until the last bit. Paula began to pace, rubbing her arms. "I don't understand why he wasn't more open."

"He's fifteen. He's male. He's confused. He doesn't know the difference between bad company and good friends."

What she had done was beginning to sink in.

"I blew it," she said after a while.

"Don't blame that on me," Zach said. His irate tone softened. "Look, he didn't steal anything, and he will get over the fact that you thought he did for—what did you tell him?"

"Five seconds."

"Yeah. And if there were other things he did do, they weren't that bad and they're in the past. Go chase real crooks."

"I don't know how I ever got along without your good advice."

"It won't kill you. You don't know everything."

"No, I don't and that's the problem. Where were you really the other night?"

"I told you—with Jake. You just don't trust other people, do you, Paula?"

"You heard what I said to Brandon. I'm a cop. Trust doesn't come easy. Especially when the man I'm dating carries a picture of another girl in his wallet."

Zach reached into his pocket and withdrew the wallet. He flipped it open to reveal the snapshot. "This girl?"

Paula cringed. She was about to feel like a fool. She knew it.

"That's my sister, Annie. I told you about her."

The ringing of Paula's phone saved her from having to respond. She grabbed it. "I have to take this. Don't go away." She stepped into the front entryway. "Hello."

Zach turned around. He sat on the stairs, elbows resting on his knees and his big hands loosely clasped. Paula mostly listened, watching him. "You going after him?" she asked the caller.

Zach looked up. She shook her head and mouthed, *Not Brandon.*

"All right. Keep me posted."

Paula slung the phone into her bag and walked back to Zach. "Move over."

"Why?"

"You once told me that the stairs were a good place to talk. Now more than ever," she said.

He scooted to the left and she took the remaining space.

"Who was that?" Zach asked.

"A detective. They found Otis's car. They're staking it out in unmarkeds and waiting for him to show up."

"And then?"

"They obtained a search warrant. But they can't arrest him. Let's see what happens."

"Nothing else to do," Zach muttered.

"Do you think we should try and find Brandon?"

Zach blew out a frustrated sigh. "Lord, girl, you are not his mother. Just leave him be. He didn't say he was hitch-hiking to China. He said he was going to visit his grandmother in the hospital. You need to start believing in the people who care about you."

"I get the point."

They sat in silence for a while. "What was that you said about me walking on water?"

"Figure of speech. Forget it. I take it back anyway."

Paula turned her head to admire his chiseled profile. The ruggedness came out when he set his jaw like that. Zach may have been mad at her, but he was right about a lot of things. So long as she didn't have to admit that in so many words, she could deal with his temporary disapproval.

"Could I get a do-over?" she asked suddenly.

Zach gave her a wry look. "Starting from when?"

"The kiss before last. When everything was perfect."

"It never was," he said. His gaze moved over her.

Paula met his eyes. Brown versus blue. Neither blinked.

"It came damn close," she said. "For four weeks, we did all right. Maybe it's only been three. You and I agree more than we disagree. And I think we have something here. Beyond the physical."

"What makes you bring that up?"

"I loved it," she said bluntly. "So did you."

"Not giving up, are you?"

Paula shook her head. "I believe you, Zach."

"All right, then," he said, smiling. "Do-over it is. Let's start right now."

Her phone rang again.

"Don't answer that damn thing," he said.

Paula ignored him and got up to take the call.

"Seriously? In the trunk?" Zach heard her say.

She stayed on the phone for a long time. He got up and went into the kitchen to make breakfast for the two of them. He slid the scrambled eggs and browned sausage onto a single platter and added a couple of Christmas cookies. When he came back out, cutlery for two in one hand and the platter in the other, she was still on the phone.

Zach sat down on the stairs and began to eat. Paula eyed him hungrily. "Listen, gotta go," she said. "Call you right back, okay?"

"I'm starved," she said to Zach.

"More than enough for two." He passed her the platter and took a cookie en route. "Who was that?"

"Detective Robson. They nabbed Otis and made him open the trunk. Guess what was inside."

"The safe," Zach said.

"You're no fun."

"Was the money in it?" Zach asked.

"Otis told them he couldn't figure out the combination. Like that would save him from a grand larceny rap."

"How's that again?"

"By his reasoning, he only stole the safe. He wasn't able to steal the money."

"Yeah." Zach reached over for another forkful of sausage. "Stupid and greedy go together. But you did good. I'm proud of you. What happens next?"

"He stays behind bars until trial or gets sprung on the way there. Same goes for the other kid, basically."

"How?" Zach asked.

"They can plea bargain, post bail, decide to become informants, get a judge to invalidate the arrest—there are lots of ways to get out of jail."

Zach took the empty platter when she handed it to him and set it aside. "Mmm. That was good," Paula said.

"Could you take yourself off the case?"

"Why would I want to do that?"

"Were you officially assigned to it?" Zach asked.

"No. But I have a personal interest in the Christmas House."

"Think about your safety, Paula. Otis doesn't know your face or anything about you. Walk away. Let Detective Robson get the glory."

"That would serve him right," she mused.

"I'm serious, Paula."

"Zach, being a cop is my job. And I love it . . . well, not as much as I used to love it."

"I'm not saying quit. Just this one case. I want those punks out of your life and Brandon's and Edith's, and I don't want them around the Christmas House ever again. You didn't make this arrest, Paula. Walk away from it."

"But—"

"Just let those two sing carols with the Orange Jumpsuit Choir and forget about Otis's case at least. Please. Christmas is coming. I want to spend every minute of it with you."

"Oh."

"Don't look so scared," he said irritably. "Figure of speech."

Paula smiled. "Don't take it back."

Chapter 22

Brandon entered the hospital and signed in at the lobby desk for a visitor's pass. He passed the gift shop. That was taken care of. He had the one he'd chosen in his pocket.

He waited for the elevators with some other people, getting on when they did and watching the numbers change as the car went up. He got off at Cardiac Care and followed the wall signs to her room.

Just outside, Brandon paused. A young nurse looked up at him from the monitor at her station.

"Is Mrs. Clayborne in there?" he asked. "I'm her grandson."

"Yes. You must be Brandon. She told me you were coming. She wanted to get herself fixed up first. She's ready and waiting. Go on in."

Brandon smiled at her. He stepped forward and knocked at the door, which was ajar.

"Gram?"

His grandmother was sitting up in a reclining bed, her hair in a semblance of a style and makeup on. The hospital gown concealed the wires to some degree, but the thin tube in her nose made him pause.

"Yes, honey. Don't mind how I look. Come here. Oh my

word. You are a sight for sore eyes. Where the hell have you been? Why didn't you call? Would you like some of this juice? You must be thirsty. I don't know what to do with you sometimes, Brandon Clayborne. You worry me half to death."

The torrent of words subsided when he leaned over and put his arms around her. "I'm sorry," he muttered.

Edith made the most of the hug. She let go of him eventually. "Reach me a tissue from the box," she said in a watery voice.

Brandon gave her a handful. She blew her nose on one and wiped at her running eye makeup with another.

"You don't know and you never will know how good it is to see you," she began. "Don't you ever stay away from home that long again. Or I will open up a can of whoopass and you won't sit down until you're my age."

"I came back sometimes," he said, sitting on the bed beside her.

"I thought you did. I noticed that some of the mess in your room got moved around now and then."

"You should be a detective, Gram."

"Let's leave that to Paula. So are you coming home for Christmas? And staying home?"

"Yeah. When do you get out?"

"Just in time."

Brandon nodded. "I want to give you an early present. You have to open it right now."

Edith brightened. "Now you're talking."

Brandon looked at her curiously. "What are you on, Gram?"

"Supplemental oxygen. It does a body good."

He shook his head in a silent laugh and reached into his pocket for his present. "Here you go. With all my love."

"Oh my. What pretty wrapping paper."

"Please. Don't save it, Gram."

"But it's my favorite color. Now what could be in this little box?"

She lifted out the turtle pendant set in silver and let it swing on the chain. "Oh, Brandon! It's wonderful! Is it hand carved?"

"Yeah. Native American. I picked it out myself." He grinned with pride. "Put it on."

"But then I can't see it," she protested.

"I want you to wear it, Gram. It's a symbol of long life and . . . something else. I forget what the lady said." Brandon thought. "Patience. That was it."

"Lord grant me both," Edith said. She clasped her hands and looked mischievously at her grandson. "And send down a double helping of the second thing."

"Aw, Gram." Brandon hugged her again. "I'm going to make it up to you."

Chapter 23

Paula and Zach had driven out to the truck stop to take care of some unfinished business. The snowy landscape outside made the no-frills interior seem even more cozy.

"You sure the food here is good?" she said, looking at the menu. The prices were rock bottom. "Everything is fried. Even the pie is fried."

"My dad is a skinny guy. He eats here all the time."

They were meeting Tyrell Bennett midway between Denver and Velde to pick up a bale of hay for a Nativity scene, the final theme room of the Christmas House.

The cook, a heavyset man in a permanently stained apron, trudged out from the kitchen.

"Heard you were here," he boomed at Zach. "So you're Tyrell's younger boy."

"Yes, sir."

The cook put a hand on his chin and looked thoughtfully at Zach. "You don't resemble him."

Zach shrugged good-humoredly. "My dad is one of a kind."

Paula smiled at the chunky cook. She couldn't think of anything to add to the conversation.

"Now who's this young lady?" the cook asked.

"This is Paula. She's a Denver police officer."

"Oh, she's the one that kid in the kitchen mentioned. Pleasure to meet you, Miss Officer. You didn't tell me her last name," he said accusingly to Zach.

"That could be changing."

"Shut up," she muttered, blushing.

"So how is Brandon doing in the kitchen?" Zach asked.

"He's a natural with a peeler. We're moving him up from apples and carrots to onions soon's he learns to handle a knife. We had him on dishwashing for a while. He didn't do too good."

Paula smiled to herself. She could have told the cook that.

"Send him out when he gets a minute."

"Sure will," the cook said. "But he likes to work. For someone who's going back to school in January, he gives it all he's got. Saving up for something. He won't tell me what."

Paula and Zach knew. Brandon was planning a Christmas homecoming for his grandmother and wanted to pay for it himself. Zach had found him the job here, way outside of Denver. Brandon was bunking in a trailer out back of the diner.

Brandon came out, wearing a white kitchen cap over his dark curls. "Hey."

"Look at you," Paula said. She would have given him a hug if he hadn't been on the job. "I understand you're getting a promotion."

"Who told you that?"

The cook wagged a finger at Paula. "Now I have to give him one." He patted Brandon on the back. "You go over there and sit with your friends. I gotta clean the grill."

"Thanks." Brandon went around the counter and slid into the booth next to Zach. "I talked to Gram today. She said to say hi to both of you."

"I'm going to go see her tomorrow," Paula said. "So tell me about your Christmas plans."

Brandon grinned. "A big honking tree, all lit up. And more presents. I have one for you, Paula."

"Here?"

Brandon nodded. "My grandma got hers early. You too."

Paula leaned over the table and gave him a kiss on the cheek. "You didn't have to do that. But thanks."

He took a tiny flat box out of his jeans pocket and slid it across to her. "It's a little one."

Paula slid a fingernail under the tape on the wrapping paper and got it open. She saw a flat silver arrow engraved in script. Paula read the words to herself.

"Thank you," she whispered to Brandon.

"You used to tell me things like that," he said. "I figured you could put it on the ring with your car keys."

"What does it say?" Zach asked. She knew he'd seen it, but Brandon didn't know she knew.

She showed Zach the engraved words without reading them aloud.

Go in the direction of your dreams.

He nodded with approval. "That's really nice," he said. "And very good advice."

Brandon seemed pleased with himself.

"I haven't bought yours yet," she told him.

"That's okay." He seemed to have other things on his mind. "Okay, so Grace is coming over early on Christmas Eve. Then her mom will pick her up, so it will be just me and Gram. I ordered a whole smoked turkey, and I already bought lots of eggnog, so she doesn't have to cook."

"Sounds great," Zach said. "You might want to round out that menu some, though. Maybe a salad, something like that."

"I could do that," Brandon said. "Good idea. So what are you two doing?"

"I don't know," Zach said. "We might go out of town."

Tyrell Bennett entered through a side door. His lean, weathered face broke into a craggy smile at the sight of his son. "Now, don't get up," he said as he came over. He took off a vintage Stetson and hung it on the hook by the booth. "So this is Paula. Very nice to meet you. Zach won't stop talking about you."

Paula pushed back her hair and sat up straight to shake the old cowboy's hand. His grip was firm. It reminded her of Zach. Hand on the reins. Gentle touch. "Very nice to meet you, Mr. Bennett."

"You can call me Tyrell. Everyone else does."

"Hi, Dad." Zach looked at him sideways.

"Is that you, son? I didn't see you at first. And you must be Brandon." Tyrell dragged over a chair and sat at the head of the booth. "Didja order, Zach? What's everybody else having tonight?"

"A damn good time," Zach said.

"Glad to hear it. I'll have a fried pie on the side."

Chapter 24

Paula shut the laptop and glanced out the window at the snow falling outside. "Okay. E-mail sent. I'm not following up on the Otis Parker case. Detective Robson will get the glory. And by the way, the cash was in the safe."

"You won't lose sleep over it. Like I said, you have it all. You're a perfect lady, a brazen hussy, and one hell of a good cop."

"Maybe not forever. What if I want to quit?"

"I'm not sure I want you to go that far," he said thoughtfully. "You have to be the only woman who could ever keep me in line."

"You might be too much man for me," she teased. "What if you get restless?"

"Do I look restless to you?" Stretched out on her sofa with his cowboy boots propped on the far arm, Zach's air of masculine assurance was a match for his lethargy.

"Not very." He looked supremely comfortable in the cozy warmth of her apartment.

"Give me a kiss," he begged. She went over to him. Zach reached a hand up into her long, flowing hair and tugged her down beside him. The tenderness turned sensual. She was a little surprised when he broke it off.

"Let's get away before New Year's," he said.

"You're on. But where?"

"I know a place. You. Me. A hundred thousand tons of snow that I don't have to shovel or plow because we're never getting out of bed."

"We haven't shared one yet," she reminded him.

He winked at her. "We did just about everything but that."

"Zach . . ."

"What?"

Paula relented. "Just tell me where we're going."

"A Rocky Mountain lodge. Exclusive and expensive. They pamper you so hard you don't have to do anything. They send the staff out to ski for you."

"Thank God."

"You'll love it, I promise. Fine dining. A ballroom. Different music every night."

"I have to like the music," Paula said.

"They have a swing ensemble, a country band, and some slow jam guys from Steamboat Springs on Mondays who never tune their guitars. We'll be gone by then."

"Let's swing."

"Great dance. I can teach you."

"Which dress do you like best on me? The wine-red or the ice velvet?"

He smiled like the devil himself. "Neither."

"Oh you."

"And," he continued, "I have something else for you. Something you really like."

"What's that?"

He put a hand in his pocket and took out something small enough to fit in his palm. "Evidence."

"I thought you wanted me to leave the job behind until next year."

In one swift move, Zach produced a ring box and opened it to reveal an oval diamond set on a simple band.

"Let this be entered into the record as evidence that I love you."

He removed the ring from its white satin nest and slipped it onto her fourth finger, left hand.

Paula just looked at it, dazzled.

"I know, I know," he said. "We only met four weeks ago. I'm asking for a year to prove that I mean what I say. I'm assuming you love me."

She pummeled him unmercifully. "I do. I probably shouldn't but I do. I do."

Zach laughed. "I like the sound of that."

He kissed her again. This time he didn't stop.